BUCKO

Center Point
Large Print

Also by Cliff Farrell and available from
Center Point Large Print:

Death Trap on the Platte

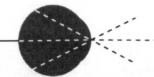

**This Large Print Book carries the
Seal of Approval of N.A.V.H.**

BUCKO

Cliff Farrell

CENTER POINT LARGE PRINT
THORNDIKE, MAINE

CHAPTER ONE

The last steer was hazed out of the pen and up the chute into a slat car on the railroad siding at Rainbow. Arch Caswell, owner of the outfit that was loading, rolled the door of the car closed and a trainman dropped the pin in place.

"Take 'em away!" Caswell yelled. "Kansas City or go bust!"

A grinning brakeman signaled the engineer. The fireman began yanking the bell cord on the locomotive. The string of filled cattle cars lurched into motion to be dragged down the siding in order to make room for more empties at the chutes.

The riders for another outfit were impatiently waiting their turn to begin loading. On the flats beyond town, more steers were being held, bearing the brands from half a dozen ranches.

It was only mid-June. The beef roundup was almost two months ahead of schedule in this northern range. Cattlemen were in a wild scramble to take advantage of market conditions that had skyrocketed the price of steers twenty dollars or more a head.

Hoof-and-mouth had quarantined all south-western and Texas beef. Drought had hit the mid-plains. Stockyards were emptying at Kansas

City and Chicago, with packing plants going idle. An open winter and an early spring, with grass greening weeks ahead of normal, had providentially placed the Rainbow ranchers in a position to reap a windfall. And it was high time that luck had turned their way after a succession of lean years.

Arch Caswell's riders whooped and fanned their hats. One or two touched off their six-shooters in the air. Caswell passed around a jug of the best Kentucky whisky and then began paying off the crew by writing out IOUs that were as good as greenbacks in every store and saloon in Rainbow.

Matthew Battles laid aside the prod pole he had been using in the blazing sun of midafternoon. He was caked with sweat-streaked dust. He had been hooked by a steer while untangling a pileup in the pens. The injury wasn't much more than a surface welt, but his shirt had been torn partly from his back. A new shirt would cost two dollars at Cy Johnson's mercantile. Two days' pay.

Rough horseplay was going on, with hats being smashed down over ears and exuberant cowboys leaping on the shoulders of others, wrestling friends to the ground. They were cutting loose after more than a month of riding beef drag from dawn to deep dusk, of throwing circle in brushy draws and on steep mountain slants, of dust and danger and bawling cattle on the cutting grounds, and the smell of burned hair and scorched flesh at the branding fires. Of bitter coffee and of man-cooked meals served at the tail gates of chuckwagons. Thirty days of not even seeing anyone in skirts.

Matt Battles was not included in the horseplay. He had been overlooked when the jug was passed around. He was the last of the crew to be paid off. Arch Caswell handed him an IOU for thirty dollars.

"There you are, Battles," Caswell said. "Thirty days' work, counting today as a full day. That's correct, ain't it?" Arch Caswell had the reputation of being a careful man with a dollar.

"Is that all you've got to say, Arch?" Matt asked.

Caswell wouldn't look him in the eye. "You might stop by the ranch next fall, if you're up that direction. Right now, I'm layin' off even regular riders for the summer, but I might be able to put on a hand for the winter."

"Sure," Matt said. "It'd be something like holding down a line camp over in the sand hills. Nobody would bother me for four, five months. And I'd bother nobody. On account of being snowed in. Or maybe it'd be a job of taking the kinks out of a bunch of those broomtails you buy each year from wild horse hunters up in Canada and try to make cowponies of 'em. And I'd pay my own doctor bills. A busted arm or leg—or a broken neck—would be my own grief."

"That's the way it is," Caswell said and walked away.

The roughhousing lost its zest. An awkward silence settled. Matt looked at the men with whom he had been riding for a month. "Sure," he said. "That's the way it is. And to hell with all of you."

One of the crew spoke. "You ought to get that chip off your shoulder, Battles." He was a big, hard-jawed, black-haired man who had given the name of Tonto Withers when he had signed the payroll.

"I like it there," Matt said. "I'm waiting for the wind to push it off."

"That'll happen," Withers said. "And it won't be the wind. God help you when it does."

Matt shrugged. He slung his saddle and bedroll over his back and walked away from the cattle pens. Tonto Withers had joined up with the roundup crew only a little more than a week previously, hired temporarily to help trail the steers to the shipping point. Like Matt, he would no doubt be laid off, now that the cattle were in the cars.

Withers had said he was from Colorado, but he had let drop a word or two that indicated he wasn't entirely a stranger in the Rainbow country. And while he might have punched cattle in the past, he didn't handle himself like a man who had done too much range riding lately.

He was a stranger to Matt but he seemed to go out of his way to work up friction between them. In a way this had been almost a blessing to Matt. To have someone stand up and lash back at him made him feel almost human again. The rest of them made a point of being respectful—and distant. They wanted no trouble with a man with his reputation.

He carried his gear into First Chance Gulch, which was what the principal street of the town was named. Rainbow had been founded on a gold strike back in the early Indian days. Cattle ranching was now the backbone of the country, but the stamp mills at some of the mines were still working on pay ore, and the lodes occasionally widened into bonanza veins that brought rich cleanups in bullion.

But Rainbow was a log and clapboard-built community where the periods of bonanza had been far between. It had seen its flood tides, but it had seen far more of the ebbs. It was now trying to fight back from one of its low points. For the greater part of the year it drowsed in its mountain meadow in the shadow of Eagle Peak, which dominated the Rainbow Mountains. Rainbow town stirred only when the miners and riders came to town with pay in their pockets.

The unprecedented early beef gather had brought a feverish flush of prosperity—and hope—to men who had been hanging on by their fingernails. Money was flowing. Cattle buyers from Kansas City and Chicago were in town and cash deals were being made for beef in the shipping pens.

Three or four temporary honkytonks under canvas had been set up to reinforce the more modest local places of entertainment. These were operated by gamblers who had come in from Denver or Cheyenne to take advantage of Rainbow's luck.

The biggest hangout was under a sizable spread of canvas, with a spangled banner that proclaimed it as the Starlight. Cowboys sporting fresh shaves and haircuts, new shirts with big pearl buttons and checkered breeches, were swarming in and out of its doors with money to spend and a thirst for excitement in their eyes.

Matt knew many of them. A few said, "Howdy!"

That was all. None stopped to talk. Many pretended they didn't see him at all. A few gazed at him with furtive curiosity.

Matt scornfully punched his weathered hat far back on his thick, dark hair. It hung there recklessly, mockingly. His dark eyes were mocking too—and challenging. A bitter, angry challenge.

He shouldered a passerby aside on the sidewalk. The man, who was a cowboy like himself, gave him a look, then walked on, refusing to make an issue of it. Once he and Matt had shared the same tarp over their blankets on stormy, wet nights in roundup camps. Now he typified the battlements of indifference, unfriendliness, and suspicion that he had endured for a year.

Once it had been another story. Once they had slapped him on the back, shouted at him to drink with them, hoorawed him as they had been hoorawing each other. Now, the only riding jobs open to him were the kind Arch Caswell had in mind. Line camps in the back country where a man could go out of his mind from loneliness. Bronc twisting with its heritage of broken bones and misery. Hunting down and branding mavericks in the canyons and brush. Tough, dangerous jobs that were filled only by men like himself. Outcasts.

Other men along the sidewalk gave him room. He cashed his IOU at a bar and entered Jake Pryer's barbershop, which was busy catering to men of the range. He waited his turn to be shorn and shaved. Jake, usually a loquacious man, didn't open his mouth while he wielded scissors and razor.

"Here's part payment on what the bank owes you, Jake," Matt said as he left the chair. He bounced a coin hard down on the marble top of Jake's work stand and walked out.

He rented a room for the night at a sidestreet

hostelry that called itself the Eagle House, but which cowboys referred to as the Bats Nest. He bought a new white shirt at the Great Western Mercantile. Cyrus Johnson, the owner, left another customer to wait on him personally. But without wasted words. Matt felt that Cy Johnson had something on his mind, but evidently decided against speaking out.

Afterward, he luxuriated in a two-bit tub in the bath shed at the rear of the Eagle Hotel. He emerged at sundown and ate steak with trimmings and hot apple pie at Sam Handley's Delmonico. A good, appetizing meal—served in an atmosphere of ice.

Mary Handley, daughter of the proprietor, was working as cashier, a position she filled on busy days. She was a small, pretty blonde with hazel eyes. Matt had grown up in this country and he and Mary Handley had attended the brick schoolhouse on Butte Creek. He had escorted her to many ranchhouse and barn dances after they had reached the age of romance. He had visioned that someday when he had made his stake they would be married.

He had gone off to greener ranges to make that stake, but had earned only a reputation as a fast and deadly man with a gun in the rustler war on the Sweetwater River down in Wyoming. But it wasn't that reputation that had come between them. Mary Handley hadn't minded being seen in the company of a man who was pointed out as a gunfighter. In fact she had seemed rather flattered by it.

She now treated him as a stranger when he walked to the desk and paid his bill. He had left a ten-cent tip on the table for the French-Indian woman who had waited on him. Mary walked to the table, brushed the coin on the floor and placed a dime of her own in its place.

Nobody in Rainbow wanted any favors from Matt Battles. Particularly his money. They said it was tainted. With blood.

He walked out of the Delmonico, his thumbs hooked in his belt. The bitter, mocking smile had deepened, twisting his lips.

Ab Russell, who enforced the law in the town limits, confronted him, looking him over. Ab wore a marshal's badge and packed a specially made .45 with a twelve-inch barrel. He preferred to "buffalo" a prisoner who resisted the order to submit to arrest by using the gun muzzle as a club, but he could be deadly and fast on the trigger if he had to draw and shoot.

Matt was not armed. Both his rifle and his six-shooter were inside his bedroll in his room at the Eagle Hotel. Ab patted his sides and armpits to make sure he wasn't carrying a hideout.

"Stay sober and steer clear of trouble, Battles," the marshal said. He was neither hostile nor friendly. Merely issuing a warning.

13

"You're wishing a dull evening on me, Ab," Matt said.

"It'd be even more so in a coffin," Ab said. "Most anything's better than that."

"I wonder," Matt said.

"Maybe so," Ab said. "Sometimes I wonder too."

The marshal walked away. He was a gaunt, stooped man who was treated with rigid courtesy, but had no close friends. He had been a law officer the biggest part of his life. It was said that he had killed at least six men. He acted now as though he walked alone. With ghosts. He was lonely.

Matt felt cold and empty inside. He was seeing himself twenty years from now, still walking like Ab on a street filled with convivial men, none of whom wanted to be in his company.

But there was at least one rift in the wall of ostracism that confronted him. Paul Wallford came down the sidewalk, walking with his usual brisk, impatient, erect stride. "Hello, Matt," he said and pulled up to chat for a moment. "How're you making out, cowboy?"

"Fine," Matt said. "Just fine, Paul."

Paul eyed him. "Don't let 'em bog you down, Matt," he said. "Keep spitting in their eyes."

"Sure," Matt said. "Sure, Paul."

Paul clapped him on the shoulder and moved on down the sidewalk. He was about the only person in Rainbow who had the sand to scoff at general opinion and be seen speaking on a friendly basis with Matt in public.

Matt appreciated Paul's attitude, even though it still surprised him. Although he and Wallford had known each other since they had been small boys they had not been particularly friendly. They had fought it out with fists as schoolboys on more than one occasion. Mary Handley had been the real cause of those conflicts.

Maturity had settled their differences. Also the fact that Mary Handley was no longer an issue. It had been announced only a month or so in the past that she and Paul were to be married.

Paul and Matt were of about the same age and height. Paul dressed well, smoked good cigars, and preferred town life to the range. He was handsome and freshly barbered. He had curly brown hair and short sideburns.

Matt watched him enter the Delmonico. From where he stood he could see the way Mary Handley brightened as she greeted Paul at the cashier's desk.

Matt turned away. Paul was the nephew of Cyrus Johnson and was his uncle's assistant in managing the Great Western Mercantile which was the financial pillar of the Rainbow country since the disaster that had closed the town's only bank.

Paul would no doubt inherit the mercantile

someday, for he was the only child of Cy Johnson's only sister. When Paul and Mary Handley were married it would be the biggest wedding the range had ever celebrated. Everybody knew and liked Cy Johnson and Sam Handley. The majority of them owed Cy Johnson more than mere friendship. He was the only one who stood between them and total ruin.

Matt walked into the Starlight. The place was crowded and noisy. A yellow-haired woman in spangles was dancing on a small stage at the rear to the music of a drum and a piano.

He ordered beer. He was still remembering the warmth of Mary Handley's smile when she had greeted Paul Wallford.

He was lifting the mug to take the first taste of the contents when a powerful hand whacked him on the shoulder with such force the mug was nearly jerked from his hand. Beer sloshed down the front of his shirt.

He whirled. Tonto Withers stood grinning at him. Withers seemed to be drunk and spoiling for a fight. "I'm knocking that chip off, Battles," he said. "I've watched you strut around like a turkey cock, snickerin' at honest folks what have lost their savin's because that tillicum o' yours went outlaw. They might be afeared o' you, but not me. I'm—"

Matt launched a fist. Withers, somehow, blocked the punch. Then they were swinging, toe to toe. Matt fought with wild, avid satisfaction. This was something tangible to strike back at, something alive and of flesh and blood that he could hit. Up to now he had been flailing only at the wind, lashing out at ghosts.

It was a barroom brawl, fast and violent, between two big men in good physical condition. It was a blur of roundhouse swings, of grunts and the thud of fists.

Matt fought in silence, but Withers kept raving at him. "Dirty thief! Damned train-wreckin' rat! You ought to be run out o' the country!"

Matt became aware of frustration. He was fighting with all the fury and skill he could summon, but none of his punches seemed to be connecting. They were mainly only glancing impacts, or were being blocked by forearms or shoulders and were doing little damage to Withers. On the other hand, while he had taken a few resounding blows to the body, he still had not been hurt.

He settled down and fought warily. Tonto Withers, he realized, was not as drunk as he had pretended. He doubted that Withers was drunk at all. At least there was one thing certain, above all. The man was exceedingly experienced at this sort of fighting.

He quit roundhousing and began feinting and jabbing. His change of tactics caught Withers by surprise. He feinted his man off balance and landed a right to the jaw that took toll. He followed with a left and right to the body. He had his man reeling.

But hands now grasped him. Something that felt like the blow of a mallet crashed on his head. He was seized by other hands. He glimpsed the tough, hard faces of three men. These were the troubleshooters, the professional gunmen and bouncers who were hired to keep order in the honkytonk.

A knee was jammed in his back and his arms were pinned to his sides. A fist smashed into his face. He lashed back with a boot, sending an opponent reeling against the bar, clutching his stomach. Another fist crashed into his face.

He saw that Tonto Withers was stretched out cold. A bartender stood over him, a rubber bungstarter in his hand.

"Throw 'em both out!" a man in a plaid coat and flowerbed vest commanded impatiently. "They're holding up the play."

Matt, dazed, was dragged through the sawdust to the door. There they pitched him across the sidewalk into the dusty street.

Withers came stumbling after him, propelled by a boot. Withers got unsteadily to his feet and stood for a moment, debating whether it was worth the punishment to go back into the place. He decided against it. He had a bloody nose and a swollen eye. He looked at Matt from his

18

undamaged eye. "You're a damned good man, Battles," he said.

Matt got to his feet. Two of the bouncers were standing in the batwing doors of the Starlight. One was toying with a blackjack—an obvious promise of what a man would be up against if he tried to re-enter the place.

Matt looked at Withers. "Why did you start that? What's your grudge?"

Withers did not answer. He turned and walked away.

Matt looked at the bouncers and the black-jack. "You earn your money easy," he said. "Sometimes."

"We're willin' to work harder," one said hopefully.

"There's always *mañana*," Matt said. "And an answer for blackjacks."

He discovered that blood was staining the front of his shirt. He sighed. His new shirt was ruined anyway. Like its predecessor, it was torn beyond repair.

He moved away. Tonto Withers had vanished. He tried to stem the blood with his neckerchief. It came from an ugly gash on his cheekbone where a fist, or perhaps a blackjack had landed. He was still a little unsteady from the effects of the blow on his head, although his hat evidently had saved him from serious damage.

He needed a doctor's stitching and medical

dressing. Blood was beginning to blind him and he discovered that he had another cut on his forehead, but it seemed superficial. In addition, he was caught in the aftermath of fight, paying toll for those violent minutes of total effort. He broke out into cold sweat and was on the verge of being sick. The blood kept streaking down his face.

He walked on shaky legs to a water trough and sank his head in its coolness. That drove some of the sogginess from his knees, but his head still swam. And the bleeding continued.

There were two doctors who had offices in Rainbow, but he had never visited their establishments, and he could not force his foggy mind to concentrate on trying to remember just where he had noticed the locations.

He turned in one direction, then uncertainly reversed his course. A few bystanders eyed him, but when he looked at them, needing assistance, they walked quickly away. They had recognized him.

He moved uncertainly down the center of the street, the crimson-soaked neckerchief pressed to his face. "Where's the nearest doctor's place?" he asked a cowboy on the sidewalk.

The man pointed. "Down the gulch a piece."

A hand touched his arm. He found himself gazing at close range at a young woman. She had nice brown eyes, and wore a light, summery dress and had a small straw hat set on hair that

20

was a rich auburn shade in the torchlight from the honkytonks. She must have come from the Mountain House, which was Rainbow's best hotel, whose entrance was nearby.

"I'll show you where it is," she said.

"I can find it," Matt mumbled. "There's no need for a lady to—"

But she was already leading him along, her fingers on his arm. "Ma'am," he protested. "You oughtn't to be going out of your way to do this."

"And you ought to stay sober, my friend," she said.

"Sober? I was never more sober in my life!"

"Is that a fact? What a life you must lead! You smell like a brewery."

"That's beer that was spilled on me. It started the fight. I didn't even get one swallow of the damned stuff before—"

"A pretty story," she said. "Here's the doctor's office and he seems to be in."

"I can take care of things from now on," Matt said. "I'm real obliged—"

His head suddenly cleared completely. He peered closer at her. "Holy cats!" he mumbled.

"There are other patients waiting," she said hurriedly. "I'll try to have him take care of you first."

Matt continued to peer owlishly at her. "All grown up into a real dazzler," he said. "I had a feeling right from the start I'd bumped into you somewhere along the trail. Nancy Chisholm. Miss Smarty Pants, acting like a real lady."

"Too much of a lady at least to stand for any more of your brand of crude humor," she said. "And grown up enough to horsewhip you if you keep it up. Come on. You're a bloody mess if I ever saw one. I'm not enjoying this, if you want to know the truth, any more than I ever enjoyed the sight of you."

She hurried up the walk to the door of the house that served as both a home and office for the medical man. Matt tried to hang back, but she kept a firm grip on his arm, forcing him along with her.

An elderly woman and a rheumy man with a cane at his side, sat in the small anteroom. Nancy Chisholm was as quick as a squirrel. She said to Matt, "Wait here." She tapped on the inner door and was admitted. She talked to the doctor and explained that emergency aid was needed and practically pushed aside the patient the doctor had been treating for some minor ailment. She did this so swiftly and with such beaming politeness that both the doctor and the patient were putty in her hands.

She ushered Matt into the inner office. "There you are," she told him. "You're in good hands now. Goodbye, and try to stay out of trouble in the future, Bucko."

She was gone before Matt could halt her.

CHAPTER TWO

Bucko! It had been a long time since anyone had spoken that nickname. A year or more. There hadn't been too many who had used it at all. Only those close to him. Very close. His father had been the first. Bucko! That had been his father's affectionate term for him. His father was gone now, along with his gentle mother. The rigors of maintaining a small ranch in the mountains had taken them when Matt was fourteen.

About the only other person who had called him Bucko had been Johnny Kidd. Johnny the Kid. A friend. A friend who had sacrificed more than life itself to save Matt from death.

Johnny the Kid. Loyal comrade, fighting man, fast with a gun, always young in heart, always loyal. And now named in posters in every law office in the West with a $10,000 reward on his head.

In the past, Nancy Chisholm had also called him Bucko on occasion. But not with affection. It had been the only tearful rejoinder she could think of to repay him for indignities he had heaped on her when they were attending the Butte Creek school as children.

She had been a lady even then—up to a point. Her mother, who was dead now, had been an

Eastern society girl who had taught her the gentler ways of life. Her father could have been elected governor if he had sought the job.

Miss Smarty Pants. Teacher's pet. The brightest pupil in school who kept being advanced grades well ahead of her age class. Fair game for the tormenting that wild kids like Matthew Battles and Johnny Kidd inflicted on her.

Now she was really a lady, cultured of voice, but still with that peppery tongue and defiant spirit that had come to the surface when the baiting went too far. Matt recalled the sharpshooting accuracy with which she could throw a rock when her temper boiled over.

With Mary Handley it had been different. Matt had been a slave at Mary Handley's feet even in schooldays. But he had been Nancy Chisholm's cross to bear. He had not seen her in more than a dozen years. She was younger than he by three or four years, but he had taken it for granted that she was married long since. He stood staring, listening to the tap of her heels on the outer walk as she made her way to the street.

The doctor, a stout, balding, tired man, was not happy now that he realized he had been browbeaten by a pretty young woman. He was even more annoyed when he identified the patient Nancy Chisholm had forced on him.

"I might have known," he growled. "I heard

there had been a brawl in that beartrap down the street. So you were in it?"

He did not attempt to be gentle as he used the stitching needle and treated Matt's injuries.

"That'll be two dollars," he snorted as he completed the task.

Matt handed over the money and said, "I'll do my best to keep clear of you from now on, Doc. You ride with a heavy spur."

He paused in the anteroom to inspect himself in a mirror. He was bandaged and bruised. He reeked of medication and stale beer. He still needed a new shirt.

Leaving the doctor's office he again visited Cyrus Johnson's Great Western Mercantile and bought a duplicate of the shirt he had purchased earlier. Again it was Cy Johnson who came hurrying to wait on him. The storeman kept shooting glances at him, and again seemed to be expecting Matt to speak. Matt was puzzled. When he paid for the shirt he felt that the owner hesitated as though about to refuse the money. Then he accepted the cash. Looking back, Matt saw the man standing watching him, thoughtfully rubbing his shiny bald pate.

Matt was uneasy. Cy Johnson had something on his mind but was afraid to speak out. Finding a dark doorway, Matt donned the new shirt and returned to the street.

His lips felt balloon-size. His left fist was

swollen. But his spirit had shrunk to the lowest ebb of his life. As low as the time he had been told that Johnny the Kid had violated the trust that had been placed in him and had helped stage a train robbery that had brought misery and disaster to many persons in the Rainbow country.

Rainbow was still bitter. And unforgiving. And Rainbow believed that not only Johnny Kidd had been in on the holdup, but that Matt himself had a hand in it. All that Rainbow lacked was legal proof, but it had already convicted him. And it had sentenced him to ostracism.

He stood debating it. Common sense told him to give up the fight for keeps and leave this range of his birth. Find a new range where he'd see a friendly face, know the warmth of conviviality when the day's riding was done. Where he wouldn't ever again have to swagger and spit in their eyes and carry a chip on his shoulder.

He ruled that out, angrily, stubbornly, as he'd always done. He'd fought this out with himself before. Many times. Flight would be a confession as far as Rainbow was concerned.

Common sense to the contrary, he knew he would stay here, come what may. He'd never bend, never break. He'd continue to scorn them and challenge them to say in words what was in their eyes. To hell with them and their unwritten verdicts, their convictions without a fair trial.

He headed for the Eagle Hotel, intending to get

his six-shooter out of his bedroll. It was a Colt .45 with a barrel dyed blue, and with perfect action and balance. It was the gun he had used that day of the fight on the Sweetwater.

Despite Ab Russell's warning, there was no law against carrying a gun in town. The custom was frowned on by the marshal, particularly when roundup pay was being spent and men were drinking. But the roustabouts at the Starlight had been armed, and with more than blackjacks. Matt had seen the bulge of shoulder holsters on them.

A man's voice spoke softly, a stride back of him. "I'm in Room 20 at the Mountain House. Ground floor on the right. Meet me there in fifteen minutes."

Matt's step slowed. The speaker overtook him, and began to stroll on past without looking his way. He was a big man in his fifties, with the weathered features and gait of a man who had spent a lot of time in the saddle. Frost was beginning to dust the tips of his hair and mustache. The badge of a sheriff was pinned to his black vest. A holster gun was slung at his side.

He was Tom Chisholm, sheriff of Cedar County. He was the father of the girl who had led Matt to the doctor's office. Tom Chisholm could have gone far in politics, but he had preferred to hold down the office of county sheriff where he could be among old-time friends. He had been

27

re-elected half a dozen times without opposition.

"Why should I?" Matt asked. He was nettled, but the sheriff's manner caused him to speak in the same cautious tone.

"It's important," Tom Chisholm murmured, still without glancing in his direction. "Maybe the most important palaver of your life. Be there. I promise you it'll be more than worth your time."

Chisholm added, "Room 20. Don't let anybody see you come to my door. Nobody! And no more talk here on the street. Somebody might notice."

Chisholm moved on ahead out of earshot. Matt presently halted, leaning against a sidewalk post. Tom Chisholm continued his stroll up the street, nodding to passersby, calling many of them by name and pausing now and then to trade banter with friends.

Chisholm had ranched on the benches below Eagle Peak in the days when a man's scalp wasn't safe. After he had been elected sheriff he had made his home and headquarters in the county seat at Cedar Springs which was sixty miles north of Rainbow on the main line of the Dakota Pacific railway. Official duties often brought him back to Rainbow, but Matt had not seen Nancy Chisholm since she had been a pigtailed school-girl.

Tom Chisholm had the reputation of never giving up when he went after a wanted man, but a year had passed since the train robbery that had ruined the bank in Rainbow, and he had failed to make an arrest. It was taken for granted that after such a lapse of time he had written off the case as hopeless.

However there wasn't any doubt in Matt's mind that the robbery was why Chisholm had made the secret request for a talk. And it really hadn't been a request. It had been more in the nature of a command. And a threat.

He watched Chisholm cross the street and return down the opposite sidewalk, then enter the Mountain House.

He moved ahead for a short distance, debating it. He shrugged and presently drifted in the direction of the Mountain House. He was moved by curiosity at least. And also by antagonism. He regarded Tom Chisholm as an opponent.

The hotel lobby and its adjoining carpeted parlor were aswarm with cattlemen and miners and fogged by tobacco smoke. An open door led to a barroom from which came loud talk and the clink of glasses.

Matt drew a few frowning glances as he passed through the lobby. He pushed open the swing doors that led to the quieter corridor that served the rooms of the guests on the lower floor. Two cattlemen with their wives were moving down the corridor. He passed by Room 20 and continued to pretend to scan numbers until the two couples had vanished into the lobby.

The hall was deserted for the moment. Returning to Room 20, he tapped on the panel and was quickly admitted by Tom Chisholm.

Chisholm closed and locked the door. "We'll talk low and soft," he said. "These damned walls might be listening."

He saw the look on Matt's face and shrugged. "Folks are always curious about a sheriff's business. They're always trying to eavesdrop."

"This is business?"

"I'm supposed to be in Rainbow to round a panel for grand jury duty," Chisholm said. "I could have done that by mail or sent a deputy. What I really made this trip from Cedar Springs for is to talk to you."

"Yeah? Now, that's interesting. Go ahead and talk."

Chisholm eyed his bandages and bruises and clucked his lips regretfully. "Sorry about the damage," he said. "We didn't figure on those troubleshooters at the Starlight getting into it."

He added, "But, at least it made it look like it was on the level. And you can't make an omelet without there being an egg or two busted somewhere along the line."

Matt was staring, frowning. "*Made* it look on the level? What are you talking about?"

Chisholm smiled apologetically. "That big cowboy who picked the ruckus with you in the honkytonk is a friend of mine."

"Tonto Withers? Well, he's no friend of *mine*."

"That isn't his real name," Tom Chisholm said. "And his real name don't matter. You'll likely never see him again. He isn't really a cow hand. Not anymore. Used to be. He hired on with Arch Caswell a little while ago as a favor to me. I asked Arch to put him on the payroll for a week or so, and that was a favor too. He's really a Dakota Pacific railroad detective. Neither him nor Arch know why I asked the favor. He knew it was some sort of a law job that it'd be better if he didn't ask about."

"Well, I'm asking!" Matt exploded. "If that fight wasn't on the level, I'd hate to be in one that was for keeps, and—"

He quit talking, remembering. Chisholm nodded. "Exactly. You weren't really hurt by him, were you? Not until the bouncers slugged you. We hadn't figured on anything like that. The fellow you were fighting is an expert at such things. He gets lots of practice as a railroad peace officer. He used to fight in the ring."

"All right," Matt said helplessly. "So it wasn't a real fight. What else do we talk about?"

"This will take some *long* talk," Chisholm said. He opened a pocket case and offered Matt a stogie. Matt refused and rolled a cigarette from his limp sack of makings. He wasn't taking any favors from anyone—least of all a law officer.

"I've been keeping tab on you," Chisholm said.

Matt gave him a twisted smile. "I've suspected that."

"I've been watching you and that chip on your shoulder. I've been getting reports from Ab Russell on how you handle yourself. Maybe you've noticed that Ab has sort of rode herd on you."

"I've noticed. I take it that all this attention means that you hoped I'd lead you to Johnny Kidd."

"Maybe. Maybe for other reasons."

Matt waited. Tom Chisholm began ticking off on his fingers the points he was making. The first joint of the second finger on his right hand was missing—the hallmark of a dally roper who hadn't got his fingers out of the way in time when he was busting a steer on the branding grounds.

"About a year ago," he began, "a Dakota Pacific express was stuck up some thirty miles east of Cedar Springs. A gold shipment from the First Security Bank here in Rainbow was in the express car safe, locked in four strongboxes. It was in bar bullion, worth one hundred and twenty thousand dollars, give or take a hundred or two."

"I know all this," Matt said. "Everybody does."

"The bullion had been bought by the bank from the Spanish Mine which had hit a rich streak of ore and had made a big cleanup. The bank was shipping the gold to a Chicago financial firm as collateral for heavy borrowing it had made. The bank had been carrying loans to ranchers and mine operators around Rainbow to help them through these tough years. Everybody was deep in mortages to the bank."

"Why are you raking all this over?" Matt demanded.

"Your friend, Johnny Kidd, was the shotgun guard on the train that night. He dropped out of sight along with three masked men who killed the engineer and fireman and blew the safe. There was no evidence that Johnny Kidd had made any effort to protect the express car from the robbers. Apparently he was in on it with the outlaws and rode away with them."

"That's impossible," Matt said.

"Why impossible?"

"Johnny wouldn't do anything like that. I know him too well to believe that."

"Better men than Johnny Kidd have gone owl hoot," the sheriff said.

"There aren't any better men than Johnny the Kid," Matt said. "He saved my life. A thing I'll never forget."

"If he wasn't in on it, why did he drop out of sight?"

"He's dead, most likely," Matt said.

"Dead men don't write post cards," Tom Chisholm said.

Matt eyed him stonily for a long time. "So you know about the post card?" he finally asked.

33

"Of course. Johnny Kidd was a fool for sending it to you. The postmaster here let me look at it before you got it. That was illegal, I know, but so is train robbery."

Matt was silent for a space. That post card. It was the one thing that had haunted him. He had destroyed it long since. But not its memory.

It was one of a legion of crudely drawn, humorous mailing cards on sale at every railroad newsstand. This one was a sketch of a cowboy being tossed from a bucking horse into a patch of prickly pear. The original bawdy inscription had been scratched out and Johnny had penned in a jest of his own. This had to do with a mishap to Matt similar to the one depicted on the post card, which had been a subject of banter between the two of them.

"I admit I don't understand it," he said. "Maybe that post card was forged."

Chisholm was relentless. "He was the one who called you Bucko, wasn't he? The only one."

"Almost the only one," Matt admitted. "But everybody knew that was a nickname for me. It wasn't a secret."

"The card was mailed at Cheyenne two weeks after the holdup. It was addressed only to Bucko here at Rainbow. As you say, lots of people knew that meant you. It *was* Johnny Kidd's handwriting, wasn't it?"

Matt was cornered. It was not only the handwriting, but the message that had been penned on the card. Nobody but Johnny could have worded it just that way.

"If Johnny was mixed up in that thing, they must have had a gun at his back," he said.

"That gold wasn't insured with the express company, contrary to common sense," Chisholm said. "Charley Moffet at the bank here, tried to save a few dollars. His shipments had been going through for years without trouble. So he took a chance. At the wrong time. You know the rest of it."

Matt knew. The bank at Rainbow had been stretched thin, and the loss of the shipment had sent it to the wall. Its affairs were still in liquidation, but many people in Rainbow stood to lose the greater part of their savings. Worse yet, many ranchers might be wiped out through foreclosure to satisfy the creditors of the bank. The present boom in beef prices might help stave off the disaster, but it would only be a reprieve at best.

"They think I was in cahoots with Johnny," Matt said.

"Yes."

"They can go to hell."

"An attitude that will end in something more serious than a honkytonk fight, as sure as the sun rises and sets."

"Did you come from Cedar Springs just to tell me that?"

"No." Chisholm inspected the tip of his stogie while he sought the proper words. "Just what would you do to try to prove that Johnny Kidd had no part in that stickup?" he asked. "Not to mention backing up your own story that you're innocent as a newborn babe."

Matt straightened a trifle in his chair. "Such as what?"

"Such as serving time in Stone Lodge?"

It was as unexpected as a punch to the heart. Matt again studied Tom Chisholm's seamy face. He found no real expression there.

Finally he nodded. "Even that, if it's needed."

"Have you got any idea of what it's like on the Hill?"

"I've been told it's no health resort," Matt said.

"What if I told you that the men who pulled the train robbery are convicts in Stone Lodge right now?"

"What are you saying? If that's the truth, then why—?"

Chisholm waved him into silence. "They were arrested at Rock Springs, down in Wyoming, about three weeks after the train job. But for another crime that they'd committed some six months earlier. A deputy sheriff in Rock Springs recognized them as being wanted up in this state for a stagecoach holdup a few months previous.

They only got a couple of hundred dollars in that job, mainly from the wallets of passengers. One of the passengers recognized them, but it was kept quiet until they could be picked up. They were extradited from Wyoming and tried over in Brule County up here. They got fifteen years each in state prison."

"But what about the train holdup?" Matt demanded.

"Nobody knew at that time that they had any connection with it. But about a month ago, the warden at Stone Lodge was tipped off by a convict snitch that they were the ones. The snitch had eavesdropped on them. The warden passed the information along to me."

"Why haven't you—?"

"Accused them? Had them tried for the robbery and for murdering the two trainmen? Where's the evidence? The word of a prison snoop? I've got to have more than that. They deserve to be hung, of course, but there's another matter I'd like to take care of."

"I can guess," Matt said. "The money."

"Exactly. A matter of one hundred and twenty thousand dollars' worth of bullion. It isn't money, but it's just as good in any market in the world. Maybe better. If that jag of stuff can be recovered, it would—"

"Recovered?"

"They had only a few dollars on them when they

were arrested. They cached those strongboxes somewhere, intending to wait until it was safe to move them. That amount of gold makes quite a load. Men just couldn't put it in their pockets, or even pack it away on their backs. They didn't have the time or the opportunity to sell it. That's certain."

He paused, then resumed. "If that gold could be recovered, it would be a mighty big help in staving off foreclosures and might even pull everybody out of the hole without being hurt much. It would be a happy thing for a lot of people around Rainbow." He paused and looked at Matt. "They might even forgive you," he added dryly.

"That would be right kind of them," Matt said.

"I want a man to go into the Lodge as a convict and try to work his way into the confidence of these outlaws," Chisholm said. "I want him to be even tougher than they are. I want a man who'll earn the reputation of being the most hardened, vicious man on the Hill."

Matt knew he was being scanned for his reaction, for indication of indecision or weakness.

"I want a man who will be able to place them under obligation to him, and to engineer an escape with them," Chisholm went on. "I'm hoping that man will be able to learn where they cached the bullion."

"Things like that have been tried before," Matt said.

Chisholm nodded. "Men have been killed trying it."

"There's one thing you haven't told me," Matt said. "Yon haven't said that Johnny Kidd is one of these men in the Lodge."

"He's not one of them. He wasn't in on the stagecoach holdup, at least. He wasn't with the others when they were arrested in Rock Springs, to the best of my knowledge."

"What makes you think I'm the man for this job?"

"I've had the idea in mind ever since I got the news from Stone Lodge," Chisholm said. "As I told you, I've kept tabs on you."

"Sure. And now that I haven't led you to Johnny, you get this new idea."

Chisholm shrugged. "You say Kidd is innocent. All the circumstantial evidence says he's guilty."

Matt got to his feet. "Go to hell."

"That's where I'm asking you to go. Into Stone Lodge."

"As a spy? A snitch?"

"These men are vicious. They're killers. Both of the trainmen who were murdered left wives and small children. If bringing men like that to justice is spying, then that's what I'm asking you to do."

Matt moved toward the door. "It's still a dirty job."

"Afraid."

Matt nodded. "Of course. But that's not the main reason."

"I don't blame you for being scared," Chisholm said. "You'd have good cause. Did I mention that the convict who eavesdropped on them was found dead not long afterward? Someone had shattered his skull with an iron bar in the laundry room."

Matt paused. "They did it?"

"Who knows? It could have been some other convict that he'd snitched on. One mistake is fatal in that business."

Matt reached for the knob of the door. "The answer is still no."

"Or is it your friend you're afraid for? Afraid that you might turn up Johnny Kidd alive and be responsible for sending him to the gallows?"

Again Matt paused. He had to face the bitter fact that Tom Chisholm was telling the truth.

"You say he's innocent," Chisholm went on. "I'm giving you a chance to prove it. You owe him something. A lot, so I hear. Your life."

Matt stood motionless. He could hear his watch ticking in his pocket. Then he stepped back from the door. "All right," he said. "I'm your man."

They studied each other for a long time. "If you try to cold deck me, Battles," the sheriff said softly, "I'll see to it that you rot in a dungeon in the Lodge as long as you live. And that will be a thousand years—or seem like it."

"How are we going about giving me this chance to double deal on you?" Matt asked icily.

"For your own sake, if nothing else, this has got to look like the absolute real thing, right from the start," Chisholm said. "The best way is to commit what looks like an actual crime, be tried and sentenced by a jury and a judge in the usual way, through due process of law."

He waved off Matt's attempt to speak. "You will hold up Cy Johnson at the Great Western Mercantile tonight and get away with what was apparently a lot of money. You'll wear a mask, but Cy will recognize you. That's so he can identify you in court. You—"

"Hold up a minute! How—?"

"It's all arranged. I talked it over with Cy this afternoon. He'll be expecting you, and will be alone. Any shooting he might decide to do will be into the ceiling after you've got away. I'll capture you later. There's a place on the trail to the Spanish Mine where we'll arrange to meet."

"Does Cy Johnson know *why* we're doing this?"

"Yes. I had to let him know how important it was. He's about the only person around here I'd trust not to talk."

Chisholm looked at his watch. "Cy closes the mercantile at eight o'clock sharp. That's less than an hour from now. He'll keep the door unlocked and stay in his office, pretending to work on the books. There won't be many people on the street in that part of town at that time. But if a citizen or two did see a masked man running out, piling a horse and high-tailing out of town it would help make the thing ring true."

"What if those same citizens took a shot at me?" Matt asked wryly. "And didn't miss?"

"As I said, you can't—"

"Bust eggs and not have to cook an omelet," Matt said. "All right. Let's hope they'll be poor shots."

Chisholm's stern lips relaxed. "I hope so too. Sit down and we'll sweat out the details, Battles."

CHAPTER THREE

Matt took a chair and sat waiting. Chisholm snuffed out his stogie. "The men you'll deal with are not only dangerous but smart. One in particular. That's Doc Diamond."

"Diamond? The Deadwood gambler?"

"Yes. And his pals, Turk Shagrue and Frank Welton. They're the kind of playmates you're to throw in with on the Hill."

"You *do* ask a lot."

The names the sheriff had mentioned were well known, Diamond's in particular. The name he used was assumed and his real identity was a mystery. It was said that he was the black-sheep of a prominent Eastern family and that he had studied medicine at a top New England university. The story went that he had fled West after killing a man in a poker game in an aristocratic Boston club.

What was actually known was that he had killed other men in quarrels over cards or women in Deadwood where he had operated a bawdy dancehall that came to be the hangout of gunmen and desperadoes.

Turk Shagrue and Frank Welton were the sort of men whose guns were for hire for any purpose. Both had served terms in prisons for rustling or manslaughter. They had drifted into Doc Diamond's orbit and had formed a dangerous combination.

Even tough Deadwood became too unhealthy for them and they had operated in Bisbee, Arizona, for a time where the big copper mines were booming. Diamond had been tried for murder there, but, as usual, had been acquitted on grounds of self-defense. He and Shagrue and Welton had also been charged with a stage holdup, but had been freed for lack of actual evidence. Eventually Bisbee also could not stomach the trio, and Diamond and his companions returned to their old stamping grounds in northern range. The last Matt had heard of Doc Diamond was that he was running a faro game in Cheyenne.

Chisholm spoke. "Do you want to pull out, after all?"

"No," Matt said.

"Good! As a matter of fact, I couldn't afford to let you go back on your word, now that I've let you in on the secret."

"That," Matt said, "sounds like a threat."

"It could be. Except for Cy Johnson and myself and one other person, you're the only man alive who knows that Diamond and his crowd are the ones I'm after."

"In other words, you're still not sure I'll play square."

"That's right," Chisholm said.

Matt eyed him sardonically. "You're not even sure I didn't have a hand in sticking up that train. That's what most people around here believe. All of them, I guess."

"You could have been in on it," Chisholm said tersely. "At the time of the robbery you were supposed to have been up in the Rainbows, trying to get yourself a bighorn. Nobody saw you. You dropped out of sight for a week."

"And I didn't come back with a sheep, did I?" Matt said. "I missed the only shot I got. This is going to keep you awake nights, isn't it? You're never going to be sure about me."

"A hundred and twenty thousand dollars' worth of gold makes quite a glitter," Chisholm said. "Treasure like that has tempted better men than you."

"Has it occurred to you that if I'd been in on the holdup that I'd also know what happened to the loot? And that I'd have lifted the cache long ago, all for myself?"

"I've thought of that," Chisholm said. "But maybe you didn't know. Maybe Doc Diamond double-decked you and didn't tell you where the stuff was cached."

He added, "*If* you were in on it. Mind you, I'm not saying I believe you were. If so, I'd arrest you. But I'm not saying I'm convinced you were hunting bighorns at the time either. Not until you offer better proof."

"The only way to get a bighorn is to hunt alone," Matt said. "You know that. Your faith in humanity awes me. Is there anything you believe in?"

"We both better believe in Cy Johnson," Chisholm said. "Maybe I have sort of lost my trusting belief in the inherent goodness of mankind. I guess I've been a law officer too long, seen the seamy side of life too much. I deal with people who'd sell their own brother for a price."

"Or their best friend," Matt said. "You really believe Johnny the Kid is alive, don't you? And that I'd sell even him to the wolves for a percentage of that bullion?"

"I believe in nothing until I see it in black or white," Chisholm said. "But a man is innocent until proved guilty. That even goes for you, Battles."

"Thanks. I'm touched."

"You apparently know it's customary to pay a percentage of any loss that is recovered in robberies of this kind," Chisholm said. "It would be worth around twelve thousand dollars to you, Battles, if you earn it."

"I'll donate it to the trusting people of Rainbow," Matt said. "There's one thing I want to mention, Chisholm. Cold-decking can run both ways. If you don't play square with me in this, I'll come after you."

46

Tom Chisholm smiled thinly. "Well, we understand each other, at least." He looked at his watch. "There's one other matter. There are a dozen or more men in Stone Lodge from around these parts. I went to the trouble of looking up their names. I had a hand in sending the most of them up. That doesn't matter. But it does matter if any of them should happen to know you personally."

He handed Matt a slip of paper carrying a list of names. "You seem to have ground this out mighty fine," Matt said.

"You should thank me. It's for your sake. It's you, not me, that might get a length of steel in his throat, like the snitch did, if they get suspicious of you."

Matt studied the list. "Here's one," he said. "Len Flowers. He used to cook for the Bar M when I was range boss there two seasons back. And here's another. Gus Willis. Up for brand blotting. He was on the Box Q payroll with me. That's all, as far as I know."

"Either of them know you well enough to call you Bucko?"

"No. I already told you Johnny was about the only one."

"But they likely knew you and Johnny Kidd were pals."

"I reckon so," Matt said.

Chisholm dug a pencil from a vest pocket and

placed checkmarks against the names Matt had mentioned. "I'll have them transferred to some other prison. Walla Walla, maybe. Prisoners are often boarded in other states when Stone Lodge gets crowded. Which it is right now."

"Why do that?" Matt asked.

"They might remember that you and Johnny Kidd were friends and mention it to Doc Diamond. He's smart. That would be enough to spoil everything."

"You seem to swing a lot of weight with the warden at Stone Lodge," Matt commented.

"There's nobody who swings more. You see, I'm going to be the new warden. Or I will be when I take over in about a week. George Anderson, who's been warden at the Lodge for years, passed away suddenly of a stroke two weeks ago. He was the one who sent me the tip about Doc Diamond being the train robbery brains. The governor asked me to take over the job. I'm resigning as sheriff of Cedar County, effective in a week."

"That will solve some problems, at least," Matt said. "I can keep in touch with you a lot easier under that setup."

"But only on vital matters," Chisholm warned. "And then you'll have to be mighty careful. Again, that's for your own sake. The prison grapevine is a fearful thing."

"You mentioned that in addition to Cy Johnson

there's another person who knows about this scheme of yours," Matt said.

"Yes."

"Who is this man? Was it the warden at Stone Lodge who died?"

"George Anderson? Originally, yes. But after his death it seemed best to take a new party into my confidence."

"Who is he?"

"Someone I trust right down to the ground."

"I'm asking you his name!" Matt said impatiently.

Chisholm hesitated. "It's better that you don't know," he finally said.

"Why is it better? It's my neck that I'm putting inside a hangrope. If I tie up with Diamond that'd be taken as proving what everybody believes already, which is that I was in on the train stickup. What if—"

". . . what if something happens to me and Cy?" Chisholm interrupted him. "That's hardly possible, but I'll guarantee that this other party will outlive us all."

Matt had to be satisfied with that for the present at least. "How do I go about this?" he asked.

"Have you got a horse?"

"Not here. My two horses are out to pasture up in Long Valley. I've been riding a Caswell string."

"Steal one, then," Chisholm said. "Stake it out

in the wagon lot back of the mercantile. Cy will forget to lock the front door when he closes up business. He'll pull the curtains in his office. You can wait until there's nobody close around in the street, then pull your neckerchief over your face and go in. The safe will be open and Cy will have an empty flour sack filled with packets of newspaper cut to the size of bills."

"Filled? How much am I supposed to be getting away with in this stickup?"

"Twenty thousand or so."

"Twenty *thousand!*"

"Cy's got that much and more on hand right now, what with this rush of business. Cattlemen are squaring their debts with him, figuring they owe it to him more than they do to the bank's creditors. These cattle buyers came here with cash in their hands to buy beef. And they're buying. Fellows like Arch Caswell, who figure they'll do better by shipping to Kansas City, might get fooled. Lucky for us, these Eastern buyers are using greenbacks. It'll be easier for Cy to imitate, and it'll be a lot easier to make folks believe you got away with it than if it was gold."

"I understand all that, but—"

"You've got to get away with enough money to interest Doc Diamond into getting his hands on it. And it'll give you a reputation that will impress him. He wouldn't have anything to do with a cheap sneak thief."

50

"So you're making me a prime grade criminal."

"No. That's your job. You've got to make yourself the toughest convict on the Hill. The hardest case the guards have to deal with. I warn you that they can make it mighty rocky for prisoners they dislike. I can't help you in such matters. You'll have to take your lumps. I wonder if you really know what you're in for?"

"It seems like I'm going to find out. How am I going to make this prison break with Diamond?"

"That's up to you also. No doubt, Diamond is already working on it. Every long-term convict is always figuring a way to bust out. You've got to wedge into it with him, or think up a scheme of your own and take him in with you."

A hand tapped on the door. "Father, when are we going to supper?" a feminine voice spoke. "It's getting late."

"In a few minutes, Nancy," Chisholm called. "I'll meet you in the parlor."

"My daughter," he murmured to Matt. "You remember her, I reckon. You were both born and raised in these parts."

Matt nodded. "I remember her. You mentioned a place where you were to capture me after I fanned out of town with a flour sack filled with paper."

"You'll head north out of town, then circle west and hit the Spanish Mine trail. Me, being a shrewd old law dog, will figure this out and pick

51

you up where the mine road fords Frenchman's Crick along toward daybreak."

Matt nodded. He knew the place. He arose and stood for a moment, weighted by doubt. "So damned many things could go wrong," he said.

Then he shrugged and added, "But it's worth a try."

Chisholm unlocked the door, waited until the hall was clear and nodded. Matt left the room, passed through the lobby which seemed more crowded and noisy than before. He saw Nancy Chisholm chatting with a group of ranch folk but she did not glance in his direction.

He stepped into the street. Many of the stores were closed, with night lamps burning. The bars and dancehalls were alive, with music spilling across the warm June night. There was no moon. The stars glittered in a vast sea of black velvet. In the mighty sky.

The sidewalks were deserted in this area. Lights still burned in the Great Western Mercantile but Matt saw that a clerk was beginning to lower the clusters of oil lamps and extinguish them in the depths of the big room. A few late customers were finishing their purchases.

Cy Johnson liked to call his place a general store. He spent the biggest part of his time back of the counter waiting on customers personally, even though he was more than well-to-do.

Many of his customers were friends who had bought salt pork, flour, potatoes—and powder and lead—back in the days when the Sioux were mighty touchy neighbors. His store had grown through the years until it sprawled over the biggest part of a city block.

The saying was that you could buy anything from a needle to a donkey engine at Cy's place and be charged only a fair price. It served as an outfitting point for ranchers and miners over a radius of two hundred miles.

But the Great Western Mercantile was far more than a store. It was the financial bulwark of the Rainbow country. Cy Johnson had carried the range on his back since the bank had gone under. He had not only extended credit for food and equipment to the ranchers, but he had borrowed from banks in Cheyenne and Denver, putting up his store as collateral, in order to keep many of the cattle outfits from being taken over by the bank's creditors.

Matt walked on past the Great Western, forcing himself to walk without haste. He went to the Eagle Hotel, got his saddle and bedroll from his room and left by the rear entrance.

Many cowponies stood at the tie rails along First Chance Gulch and he debated the advisability of helping himself to one, but decided that it might be too dangerous. He made his way to the flats beyond the shipping pens where the *remudas* of the crews that had shipped beef were being held in rope corrals.

He located the Caswell string, identifying it by the chuckwagon that Arch Caswell had brought to town with the beef gather. The wagon was buttoned up and dark. There was no nighthawk on duty, for the horses were still working on the generous portion of hay that had been forked into the rope enclosure. All of Caswell's crew were in town celebrating the finish of the roundup.

Matt located the best horse in his own personal string that he had ridden on roundup. He roped it out of the corral, saddled and mounted. The horse was a strong-mouthed sorrel with a world of endurance and hadn't been worked for a day or two. It bucked a little, its customary protest, then settled down.

He had left his rifle in the bedroll which was lashed on the horse, but had donned his holster and six-shooter. He flipped open the cylinder of the .45, shook out the shells and dropped them in his pocket. He placed the empty six-shooter back in the holster.

He rode to the dark open lot back of the mercantile and tethered the horse to one of the gnawed tie rails. He walked to the street and scouted the store.

The curtains were drawn in the main windows of the mercantile. Only the glass panes in the double doors of the entrance were uncovered.

Lamplight showed back of the curtained windows in a front corner of the store where Cy Johnson's office was located.

The sidewalk was deserted, except for a drunken cowboy who was clinging to a post on the opposite sidewalk and an elderly woman who was hurrying home with a market basket on her arm. Both were so distant they offered little danger.

Matt pulled his neckerchief over the lower part of his face, drew the empty pistol, walked quickly up the plank steps to the door of the mercantile.

The door opened when he pressed the thumb latch. He stepped in. The main room was dark, shadowy, and deserted. It was heavy with the mingling aroma of apples and calico, of potatoes and spices, of leather and casks of cheese.

To Matt's right, the door to Cyrus Johnson's lamplit office stood open. Cy Johnson sat at the big, scarred table that he used as his desk. His back was to the door and he seemed to be intent on a ledger over which his head was bent. A curl of tobacco smoke arose, evidently from a cigar he was holding out of sight in his left hand.

The door of a small inner office opened beyond the table. Matt could see the big iron safe there. Its door was agape.

"All right!" Matt said hoarsely, stepping into the office. "This is a stickup!" He said it lamely, feeling sheepish.

Cyrus Johnson remained motionless and queerly bent over the ledger, his right arm resting on the desk. His bald pate was pasty white in the lamplight.

He did not move! A sudden, chilling premonition drove through Matt. He moved closer to the silent figure.

"Mr. Johnson?" he whispered.

There was no response. No movement except the slow, rising spiral of fragrant tobacco smoke.

Matt's next action was instinctive. He holstered his gun and touched Cyrus Johnson. He was touching a body that was still warm, but it was that of a dead man.

It began to slide, soddenly. Matt instinctively seized a shoulder, attempting to prevent the body from slumping off the chair to the floor.

Cyrus Johnson was a big, pear-shaped man. His bulk was too much for Matt in his present position, and he pivoted around the chair, placing his left hand on the desk to brace himself in order to steady the weight of the dead man upright in the chair.

Sharp pain darted through him. He had placed the heel of his left hand on the end of a live cigar that had been, not in Cy Johnson's hand, but in an ash tray on the desk.

He forgot the injury as he stared at an object that had been driven into Cyrus Johnson's back. It was the ugly spike of a miner's candlestick, a piece of equipment made of heavy iron that could be wedged in the crevices of rock in mine tunnels. These items were part of the stock in the outer room and several of them were on display in a rack just outside the door of the office.

The spike had been driven almost through Cyrus Johnson's body—through his heart. Blood was thickly wet on his back. It formed a pool at his feet. It no longer flowed, but it was almost as though he was still alive, for death had been recent. Very recent. Only minutes ago.

Matt, still bracing the body with his right hand, looked at the open safe. Its contents were scattered. Papers and ledgers had been thrown about. A few bags of small coin and silver dollars lay on the floor. If the safe had contained money in any sizable amount there was none in sight now.

Matt's mind kept mechanically following the pattern that had brought him here. He was supposed to make off with a flour sack filled with packets of fake bills. He looked around in search of the sack. He could not locate it.

What had happened? He kept expecting Cyrus Johnson to start talking and explain this. He couldn't believe that the mercantile owner was dead. Not really dead. This had not been a part of Chisholm's plan. It could not be a part of it.

He straightened. A man's voice, high-pitched with excitement, was shouting in the street, "Holdup! Holdup! At the Great Western!"

A space of silence came. It was as though an alarm bell had sounded one penetrating note and the clapper was swinging ponderously to strike the next strident alarm.

"What happened, Mr. Johnson?" Matt breathed. "Who did this?"

There was no answer. There never would be an answer from Cyrus Johnson. The shrill voice pealed out again in the street. "The mercantile is being robbed! Holdup! Holdup!"

Matt exploded out of his stunned state. This was more than robbery now. This was murder. The murder of the best-liked man in the country. He would never live to explain, if they came through the door and started shooting.

He left the office and raced back into the dark recesses of the main storeroom and found his way to a rear door. It was locked from the inside and he had a bad moment when a ponderous bolt resisted. Then it yielded and he raced into the starlight, the great free starlight.

In the next moment he was on the horse and riding away through the back areas of the town, hearing the rising excitement in First Chance Gulch.

It was not until then that he realized that the neckerchief had slipped down from his face—

probably while he was in the store. The chances were that he had been recognized.

He spurred the horse through the outskirts of the town, past the last goat yards and garden patches and rickety shacks. At a distance he pulled up, listening. He could still faintly hear the tumult in the town. And then the drumming of hoofs. Riders were already astride.

The hunt was on! And there were plenty of hunters, what with the roundup crews being in town.

He left the trail and took to the open country, keeping to the cover of brush and the deep shadows of the ridges. He cut westward, then north for a few miles, following rough country along the base of Eagle Peak, then headed south toward the trail to the Spanish Mine.

Tom Chisholm, according to plan, would be waiting for him at the Frenchman's Creek ford along toward daybreak. He rode slowly, cautiously, for he had time to spare. It was well past midnight when he topped the last ridge, with the creek only a rifle-shot away, nestled in its fringe of brush.

But the night brought sounds. The drumming of hoofs. Riders were on the mine trail, coming from the direction of town.

He swung away from that danger. He now came to full realization of what he was up against. The chances were that they'd shoot first, or maybe use a hangrope in a hurry if they caught him. The chip he had carried on his shoulder suddenly became a weight that would kill him. He was the wild one, the go-to-hell pal of Johnny the Kid. A gun swift, a man they believed was in cahoots with outlaws.

He pulled up and dismounted in order to rest his horse and to give him time to think. He became aware of the aching pain of the cigar burn on the heel of his left hand. He nursed the injury absently while he tried to plan his next move.

He was sure the manhunters were covering all the trails. They would be sending armed men to the passes over the Rainbows, no doubt, and down every road to the east and south. That was about all they could do until daybreak.

When dawn came there'd be a hundred riders, or more, ranging the country. They'd be sure to pick up his tracks. Sooner or later they'd corner him.

Tom Chisholm was his one hope. He had to get to the sheriff before the searchers found him with a hangrope. He ransacked his mind and came up with only one plan that offered possible success. And that was because of its boldness.

He mounted and headed east toward the one place they were least likely to expect to find him. In town. In Tom Chisholm's own room at the Mountain House.

He avoided the trails and followed rough

country, forcing his horse along deer paths through thickets on treacherous slants. It was perilously near daybreak when he crossed Butte Creek not far from the outskirts of town.

He circled cautiously to the flat where the Caswell *remuda* was held and turned the horse he had appropriated back into the rope corral to rejoin its companions. He hid his saddle and bedroll under a stack of railroad ties near the shipping pens.

He scouted First Chance Gulch from a building corner. The street was black and deserted. The gambling houses, which normally never closed their doors when the roundup crews were in town, were closed now. Cyrus Johnson's murder had laid a bitter pall over the town.

He walked to the Mountain House. Its lobby was vacant, with only a night lamp burning over the clerk's desk. Newspapers were scattered on the carpet and ash trays were overflowing with dead cigars and brown paper cigarettes. A ghost had appeared, halting the party. The guests had rushed away from the festivities to ride with vengeance in their hearts.

He tiptoed across the lobby and made his way down the hall to Room 20. He listened at the door, but heard nothing. He tried the knob, hoping against hope that the sheriff had failed to lock the room when he had left.

The door opened at his touch. The room was

dark, the blinds drawn. He closed the door softly and searched a pocket for a match. Finding the packet, he ignited one.

"All right, Battles," Tom Chisholm's voice said. "The lamp's there on the stand by the bed. Light it."

CHAPTER FOUR

The sheriff sat in a cane-backed rocking chair, a six-shooter in his hand. He was fully dressed, even to the spur on his right boot.

"Thank the good Lord!" Matt sighed. He lifted the chimney from the lamp, touched the match to the wick and adjusted the flame and replaced the chimney.

Tom Chisholm sat rigid and grim, eying him. Matt looked at Chisholm's gun. "Do you need that?" he asked.

An odd expression of mingled doubt and distrust held Chisholm's face. "You couldn't resist temptation, could you, Battles?" he finally said.

Matt didn't answer for a moment. "Are you trying to say you think I killed Cy Johnson?"

"What else? Thirty thousand dollars is a lot of temptation."

"*Thirty* thousand dollars?"

"I don't suppose you had time to count it. What did you do with it?"

Matt suddenly began to laugh harshly, jeeringly. "I'll be damned! How dumb can a man be. So that's the way it is!"

"What do you mean?"

"What are you going to do now, Sheriff? Kill

me, so that I can't ever get a chance to tell how you played me for a fool?"

"Played *you* for a fool?" Chisholm snorted. "You surely haven't got the brass to try to say that I—"

". . . that you got there ahead of me?" Matt asked. "Exactly. You're the one who let me walk into a frameup you had set for me. It's clear enough now."

"Of all the crazy—!" Chisholm began.

"This whole thing was a deadfall, wasn't it? That yarn about Doc Diamond and all the rest of it was only bait for me so that I'd take the blame for something you'd figured out. You're the one who couldn't resist temptation. You knew that safe was loaded with money. You told me so yourself. And you're the one who got it."

Chisholm, stunned, started to speak, then checked it. He sat glaring, the .45 cocked and half-raised. Slowly his fury faded. "Why did you come here?" he finally growled.

"I was fool enough to think you were the only man who could help me," Matt said. "There's a bullet or a rope waiting for me everywhere else."

Chisholm let the gun sink into his knee. "If you didn't do it, who did?" he asked.

"You're the only man I can think of."

"Bosh! I was with my daughter, eating supper at the Delmonico. I went there with her right

64

after I finished talking to you. I can prove it by a dozen witnesses."

Matt was almost convinced. And something else was also suddenly clear to him. "You're not *sure* that I killed Cy Johnson," he said. "Are you? Otherwise you wouldn't be here. You expected me to show up here—to get in touch with you."

"Maybe," Chisholm conceded. "When you stepped through that door it was a big point in your favor. I sneaked back here, just on a hunch. The rest of the boys think I'm still out in the brush, hunting you."

"How about this mysterious third party you said you had talked to about your scheme?" Matt demanded. "Maybe he's the one who saw his chance to feather his nest and murdered Cy Johnson."

"Impossible!" Chisholm snapped.

"Why impossible? You just mentioned the right word. Temptation. Every man is human. Why is he—?"

"I say it was impossible. If you didn't kill Cy—and mind you I'm not saying you didn't—then it could have been anyone. Maybe it just happened to be bad luck that you went in there masked at the wrong time. A lot of people knew Cy had plenty of cash in that safe last night."

"Speaking of cash, Cyrus Johnson was supposed to have a sack waiting for me, filled with packets of fake money," Matt said. "I was plenty excited when I found him dead with a spike in his back, but I don't recall seeing anything like that around."

Chisholm rubbed his chin, frowning. "That's strange. I figured you'd taken the sack and got rid of it. All I know is that Cy had cut out the packets of fake bills. I found a lot of scraps from newspapers in the stove that were left over from the job. Cy hadn't got around to burning them."

"What happened to the sack, if there was one?"

"Whoever got away with the real stuff got rid of the fake bills too."

"Where do we go from here?" Matt asked.

"Maybe this might be a help to us, even if it won't help poor Cy."

"What do you mean—help?"

"If you're on the level, Battles, this will make it look all the better reason for you being in Stone Lodge."

"You're not trying to ask me to still stand for being sent up on this holdup charge? Man, don't you know it's more than that now? It's murder!"

"All the better. Lifers generally are mighty desperate men. It'll help get you in with Doc Diamond, maybe."

"You're forgetting one little point," Matt said. "They hang men for murder. Hang them!"

"You can plead not guilty," Chisholm said. "You can say it was a case of mistaken identity. That always gives a jury pause for thought. After all, the identification was mighty thin. Only one witness."

"That must be the man who spotted me from the street," Matt said. "Who was he?"

Tom Chisholm hesitated. "Paul Wallford," he said. "Cy's nephew. He had forgotten something he'd left at the store, and was on his way back to pick it up. He said your neckerchief slipped as you were running away and he recognized you."

He peered closer at Matt. "Paul was a friend of yours, wasn't he?" he added.

"He was about the only man in Rainbow who didn't feel like it was a disgrace to be seen speaking to me," Matt said bitterly.

"There's only Paul's word. Any lawyer can point out how easy it was for him to be mistaken. Juries don't like to send a man to the gallows if there's the least doubt in their minds. The worst you'll get is life."

"Life? My God! You talk like—"

"You're safe enough, Battles. I'll sort of let the judge and prosecutor know that it'd be better not to hang you until we find out what you did with the thirty thousand dollars."

"And what if the judge throws you in jail too, for contempt of court by trying to influence him?"

"You'd still be safe enough. If anything went wrong, I'll explain the whole thing and you'll be exonerated."

"You don't really think I'd be fool enough to be tried for a murder I didn't commit?" Matt said.

"You're going to be tried whether you want to or not," Chisholm said tersely. "I still ain't so danged sure you didn't do it."

"You'll likely be sent up with me, if I tell how you talked me into perpetrating a crime," Matt said.

"Don't forget that if you tell that story to anyone, you'll be ending all chance of ever finding out about your pal, Johnny Kidd," Chisholm said.

That stopped Matt. Chisholm saw that and nodded. "I'll make a deal with you, Battles. Go through with this and I'll stand back of you to the limit if you're on the square. I'll see to it that whoever killed Cy Johnson is brought to cases. Bill Varney, my chief deputy, is going to get the temporary appointment as sheriff when I step out. Bill's a good man. He'll get the guilty man sooner or later."

He added, "You've got nothing to lose."

"Nothing but my life," Matt said.

But he was thinking of Johnny the Kid. And the debt he owed Johnny. Or Johnny's memory. He was recalling the day he and Johnny had stood facing half a dozen paid gunmen in the rustler war down on the Sweetwater. That had been a time of blazing guns, a peak moment in a man's life.

He and Johnny could have crawled and welched and avoided the fight. The odds were so high against them they had believed that their last minute was at hand. Neither had weakened. Johnny, with his ginger-red hair, his peppery spirit, had laughed at the odds, laughed at death and had told the opposition to do its worst.

They had shot it out. He and Johnny had come out of it alive. They had bullets in their bodies and had lain at the point of death for days. But they had won that battle also and had lived. Two of their opponents had been killed in the fight. The others, two of them wounded, had dropped their guns and had quit.

He remembered other and better events in which he and Johnny had figured. Episodes that were more in keeping with their real way of life. Such as the time they had gone swimming in a railway water tank on a blistering July day when the buffalo grass was so dry it crackled under foot. The wooden tank, built like a big barrel, had burst because of their activities and they had been washed, head-over-heels, into the sagebrush amid a torrent of water like two naked mermen, with the amazed passengers of a halted train staring from the windows.

Then there had been the time they had ridden into Rainbow with a few chunks of rich gold ore, and with elaborate secrecy had the specimens assayed at Milt Geiger's shop. And how they had let the report of the assay leak out.

They had half of the male population, and some of the opposite sex also, keeping close track of them, plying them with free drinks or free meals in an effort to wheedle from them the location of their "strike."

The ore, of course, had been a keepsake that Johnny had inherited from his father who had been a prospector in the past. Its origin was forgotten.

But, above all, Matt was remembering the day he and other riders for the Box Q outfit had been fighting a grass fire that threatened to wipe out the summer graze for miles. He and Johnny had been dragging the ax-split half of the carcass of a steer by their saddle ropes along the line of the burning grass. The bloody weight of the beef was subduing the blaze so that men on foot with wet gunny sacks and blankets could follow and complete the snuffing.

It was hot, dangerous work. They struggled in heat and blinding smoke, with clumps of dry tumbleweeds exploding like powder around them.

It was Matt's horse that had fallen into a brushy gully, pinning him down, just as the fire reached the rim. He recalled that moment as vividly as though it was again happening to him. As always, cold sweat sprang out on his forehead. For he had expected to burn to death.

Johnny had pulled him out. Johnny had left his horse and had leaped into the gully on foot. With brush bursting into flame around him, Johnny, with a strength both had talked about with awe afterward, had rolled the dead horse from him and had dragged him through a flaming gantlet to safety.

They had been hospitalized for many days that time also. Matt still carried the scars on his body. But Johnny the Kid had scars that went deeper. Johnny's right hand no longer looked like a hand when he got out of the hospital. He had marks on his face that made an old man of him in appearance—and in spirit. He had a limp that would go with him to the grave.

Johnny had been one to laugh and sing and swing the girls at the range dances. He had usually been among the top money men at roping and riding at the rodeos, and had won more than his share of prizes in the turkey shoots.

Johnny had quit riding, for he could no longer hold up his end at dabbing a loop over a spooky calf and delivering it hog-tied at the branding fires. He quit singing and dancing. And he quit laughing.

But he could still pull the trigger of a buckshot gun with a finger that looked like a claw on his maimed hand. He had taken on a job that he had held in high scorn in the past, that of shotgun messenger on express cars—a lonely, monotonous task where the spirit was dulled and the soul of a born cowboy was not free.

Johnny had nursed a broken heart back of an outward indifference. Matt, knowing him better than any man alive, had known heartbreak also. For this was the price Johnny the Kid had paid for loyalty to a friend. But, since the fire, Matt had never called him Johnny the Kid. There was too much hurt in that. Too many memories of other, great days.

Tom Chisholm had sat in silence, watching, as Matt's mind carried him back through these memories.

Matt drew a long breath. "All right," he said. "Come what may, I'll go through with it."

Chisholm offered his hand. "Do we shake on it?"

Matt refused. "We'll shake when I'm sure you'll keep your word."

Chisholm smiled wryly. "You're a hard man, Battles. Harder than I expected." He added, "You'll need to be."

"How hard did you expect me to be?"

"I've heard about that gunfight on the Sweetwater."

"That was quite a while ago. I'm older. Wiser."

"Sure," Chisholm said. "And lonelier. I know how it is. I've had to shoot a few men in my time.

That's what a rep as a gun swift does for you. People grow afraid of you. They're polite. Too much so. Too friendly, too eager to act as though you're just like them. But you're not. You're a loner."

Matt was surprised. "So you know about that?"

"I know," Chisholm said. "Ab Russell knows too." Then he put aside the ghosts that haunted him. "You better stay here in this room. Maybe until dark tonight."

Before Matt could protest, he added, "Some of the boys might try to get ugly if they found out you were here. I've got to pull out now and start acting like I'm still interested in hunting you. But I'll stay close to town, just in case somebody gets wise and starts trouble."

"Trouble?"

"The kind with thirteen knots," Chisholm said. "But I doubt if they'd waste time tying that many knots in a hang noose. Come dark, we'll weasel out of town and make it to the county seat. Things won't be as hot at Cedar Springs. I've got a strong jail there and a couple of deputies who are tough enough to discourage anybody with ideas. I don't put any confidence in that crackerbox they have here that Ab Russell uses to sober up drunk cowboys. You'll be safer back of strong iron bars."

"That's hardly a cheerful thought," Matt said.

"You better let me have your gun."

"No. It happens that it isn't loaded right now, but I'm going to correct that."

"How will it look? You're supposed to be my prisoner."

"It'll look a mighty sight better to me than being dragged out of here by a mob without a chance for my life."

Chisholm shrugged, conceding the point. "Hungry?"

"Now how would I know? Man alive, do you think I've had time to worry about my gizzard?"

"You ought to have something under your belt. You've had quite a night of it, and it might not be all over with. I'll have Nancy get some fodder for you after the kitchen opens for breakfast." Chisholm peered around the window blind. "That won't be long. It's almost broad daylight."

He saw the frowning question in Matt's face. "Don't worry about Nancy," he said. "She's been the daughter of a sheriff too long to be surprised by anything I ask her to do. She can have her Aunt Aggie fetch a tray to her room, and then sneak it in here when the sign is right."

Matt's frown deepened. "Her Aunt Aggie? Do you mean Mrs. Wallace, the housekeeper here at the hotel?"

"Aggie's my sister. I thought you knew that. She's been the housekeeper here ever since she was widowed fifteen years ago or so."

Matt nodded. "I'd forgotten. She *is* your sister,

isn't she. I seem to be putting my faith in the whole Chisholm family."

"Aggie won't talk, even if she suspects anything," Chisholm said. "It's not unusual for guests to have their breakfasts brought from the kitchen to the rooms. That's one of Aggie's jobs. Nobody will know who it's for."

Matt was dubious, but had to accept Chisholm's assurance. Chisholm arose, sighing and favoring tired bones. "Keep the door locked so nobody can pop in on you," he warned.

He left the room. Matt turned the key in the lock. He heard Chisholm tap on the door of the adjoining room. Nancy Chisholm evidently had been awake and expecting something like that, for she responded quickly. He heard them talking in muted whispers for a moment.

After that, Chisholm walked quietly down the hall and left the hotel. The adjoining door closed softly.

Daylight framed the window blinds with slits of gray and filtered through cracks in the oiled surfaces. Matt blew out the lamp which was no longer needed. The town lay silent after its night of excitement. As silent as Cyrus Johnson on his slab in Mort Dexter's undertaking rooms.

That silence was broken by the report of a rifleshot. Matt hurried to a window and peered around the blind. The echoes of the shot had died. The world was gray in the dawn. Colorless.

The window overlooked the hotel's hitch lot, which had a corral and barn at the rear. Matt had a slanting view across the lot into the street.

Tom Chisholm was sprawled in the dusty wagon ruts of the street. His hat lay nearby.

Matt heard Nancy Chisholm begin screaming in the next room. Her outcry faded. For her father had moved. He rolled over and over until he reached the shelter of the lip of the plank sidewalk opposite the hotel. He lay there, his .45 in his hand, swinging the muzzle in search of a target.

He did not fire. He could find no opponent in sight. Matt could see no mist of gunsmoke, no movement. The shot must have come from inside a building, or perhaps from back of the false fronts that adorned many of the roof tops.

The town stirred. Heads appeared at open windows. Tom Chisholm scuttled to the better protection of a store doorway. He had played the Indian trick, pretending to have been killed in order to delude the bushwhacker.

Men came into the street, asking questions. They and the sheriff searched the buildings and combed through the barns and sheds of wagon yards in the background, any of which might have sheltered the rifleman. The hunt was futile.

"A drunk, most likely," the sheriff said as he returned to the street and retrieved his hat. "Full of brave-making whisky and trying to be tough by dusting the hat of a peace officer."

Presently Chisholm rode out of town, mounted on a fresh horse to continue the pretense at manhunting. Matt, peering from his vantage point, could see the bullet hole in the peak of the sheriff's hat.

The town quieted. The sun came up. Wood-smoke rose from kitchen chimneys. Freighters began pulling out for the mines with their creaking wagons and jerkline strings. Early rising guests in the hotel opened and closed doors.

Matt caught sight of himself in a small mirror. He was haggard, unshaven, and had a hunted look. The beating he had taken from the Starlight bouncers had not helped his appearance. He ached in every fiber. A blister had formed on his hand where he had encountered the live cigar on Cyrus Johnson's desk. But these things were insignificant in comparison to his mental turmoil.

The walls were thin. He heard Nancy Chisholm open the door of her room and intercept the floor maid, whose voice was that of a slow-witted Indian woman. Nancy asked the maid to summon the housekeeper.

Agnes Wallace soon came to the room and Matt could hear her talking to her niece in low tones. He pressed an ear to the wall. And was rewarded.

"And make it three eggs, Aunt Aggie," Nancy Chisholm was saying. "Four would be better. And a full-sized steak. And plenty of toasted bread. With some of your plum jelly."

Agnes Wallace left and Matt had the impression she was muttering dubiously to herself as she walked past his door. He suddenly realized that he *was* hungry. Very. Steak and eggs! That sounded the first note of reality in hours. All the rest of it had been something out of a nightmare. It steadied him. He began thinking more clearly. But thinking was of no help.

He could only ride along with the play and trust to the discretion of Tom Chisholm's two women kinfolk. He paced the room.

After a time, he heard Agnes Wallace return. From the sounds he knew that a tray of food was being delivered to Nancy Chisholm in her room. He even detected the aroma of coffee and steak. Or perhaps that was only his imagination.

The housekeeper left. There was a long delay, for a steady procession of passersby moved up and down the hall. Finally the opening came. He unlocked the door at the sound of a hurried knock and Nancy Chisholm came rushing in, bearing a cloth-covered tray.

He closed and locked the door. "I was beginning to think you'd never get here," he said.

"Keep your voice down," she warned. "These walls must be made of cardboard. And I must say that's an ungrateful welcome, after the way I fibbed to Aunt Aggie. I told her I had a very hearty appetite this morning."

"Did she believe you?"

She shrugged. "No. She didn't ask questions, but she's probably guessed who this breakfast is for. You needn't worry. It isn't the first time my father has held a prisoner here in the hotel without letting the public in on it."

She poured coffee and helped herself to toast and jelly. "Don't mind me," she said. "Feed hearty. I'm afraid the steak and eggs are cold, but that can't be helped."

"You can't spoil an egg," Matt said as he pitched in. "Not even by making an omelet out of 'em."

She watched, fascinated. "Being wanted for murder does not seem to impair your appetite, at least," she commented. "But then you always did have a hungry look, Bucko. Or should I call you Skinny, like I used to?"

"Let's not start casting names again," he said. "We're supposed to be grown up." He added, "You don't seem to be worried about being alone with a man wanted for a killing."

"I used to be able to outrun you," she said. "I believe I still can. In addition, I'm not exactly defenseless."

In her hand appeared a derringer. It was a double-barreled weapon of .50 caliber, deadly at close range. She returned it to its hiding place in the sleeve of her blouse.

"I'm used to being around criminals," she said.

"You have the advantage of me," Matt commented.

"I act as my father's secretary," she said. "I work in the jail office at Cedar Springs. I'm sworn in as a deputy sheriff."

"I could have grabbed you and that sleeve gun half a dozen times," Matt said.

"But you didn't know about the sleeve gun until now, and you'd have got a hole blown in you. Why didn't you try it?"

Matt dropped the subject. "Who took that shot at your father?"

She peered. "Are you saying it was really aimed *at* him?"

"It knocked his hat off. What would you say?"

"I didn't know the bullet really did that. I thought it was as Dad said, some drunken man trying to show off."

Matt saw that she was much upset. "He's been shot at before," she said. "Lots of men hold grudges against law officers who have arrested them. I've always been afraid . . ."

She didn't finish it. Matt told himself that the man who had tried to kill her father was the same person who had murdered Cyrus Johnson. And that person must be the third party the sheriff had taken into his confidence in the plan to recover the train robbery loot.

It seemed logical to believe that this person had seen his chance to feather his nest and let Matt take the blame. The killing of Cyrus Johnson probably had not been a part of the robbery plan. After that crime had been committed, it had led to another—the attempt to silence the sheriff who was the only person who could reveal the identity of the murderer.

All that was missing, as far as Matt was concerned, was the name of this third person, this killer. Tom Chisholm would know.

At that point Matt found that he had stepped off into space and was left without an inch of ground to stand on. Chisholm was an intelligent man and surely would have arrived at the same conclusion. But he had not acted. Why?

Matt's theory fell in ruins. With a harsh jolt he was suddenly certain he knew the real identity of the mysterious third party to Chisholm's compact of secrecy. And that person was not the one who had tried to murder the sheriff. For the third party was standing there before him. Nancy Chisholm.

"Something wrong?" Nancy Chisholm asked. "You look like you just hit your thumb with a hammer."

"It's worse than that," Matt growled. "A fine, big, bright idea just blew up right in my face."

"Think hard. You might get another in the course of time."

"You look like a lady on the surface," Matt said, "but you're still Miss Smarty Pants."

"Now, who's casting names? If you're through licking the platter clean, I'll take my departure with the empty dishes."

She paused, listening. The sound of men's voices came from outside the hotel. An ominous, deep rumble.

Matt strode to the window and peered around the blind. Men were gathering in the hitch lot. More were pouring in from the street. All of them were staring directly at the window and at his eye at the opening.

"There he is!" a man yelled. "I told you I was sure it was him I had spotted a while ago, peeking out like a badger from that window. Chisholm's been leading us on a wild goose chase. He must have caught the filthy devil some time last night and has been hiding him out, waiting a chance to sneak him out of town before we can get our hands on him."

"Murderer!"

"Killer!"

"Come on, boys," the first man yelled. "Let's get him! Fetch a rope!"

The speaker was Paul Wallford. Many members of the group were cowpunchers with whom Matt had ridden. All were dusty and saddle

82

worn, having just returned from a night of man-hunting.

Like Wallford, many of them had been his friends. Now they were members of a lynch mob.

CHAPTER FIVE

Matt tore the blind from the window and stood there for the mob to see. "You're wrong!" he shouted. "I didn't—!"

He was drowned out by a wild roar of rage.

Paul Wallford seemed to be the firebrand in the mob. He was standing, a fist clenched, shouting something, his face aflame—shouting for vengeance for his uncle's death.

Wallford led a rush toward the door of the hotel and the mob followed him. Matt heard them come thundering down the corridor.

He drew his pistol and loaded it. "Get out of here while there's time!" he said to Nancy Chisholm.

Instead, she snatched the .45 from his hand. "No!" she said. "No!"

She opened the door and stood facing the men who jammed the hall. She cocked the six-shooter and lifted it.

The shouting faltered and died. Matt moved to her side, but she pushed him back. She leveled the gun on a big, gray-haired cattleman who was in the vanguard of the mob. He was Del Ordway from Long Valley, whose dominating size and penetrating voice made him a natural leader. Paul Wallford had drifted into the background.

"Don't come a step farther, Mr. Ordway,"

she said. "Or any of you. If you do I'll begin shooting."

Matt again tried to drag her away from the doorway, but she shook off his hand with a lithe and savage twist of her body.

"Keep away from me, Mr. Battles," she said, "or I'll shoot you, too."

Del Ordway looked like he wished he was anywhere but here. "Now, now, Miss Chisholm," he began, his voice running up the scale as he tried to make himself smaller. "You just stand aside and let—"

"This man is a prisoner who will be tried in court," she said. "I'm a deputy sheriff, sworn to uphold law and order. You know what my father would do if you tried to take a prisoner away from him. I'll do the same."

Matt felt that if it really had been her father who was blocking the door, the hall would have been the scene of carnage, for these men would have shot their way into the room to seize him. But, coping with a young, ashen-lipped woman whose eyes were dark with determination, was something else again.

Suddenly it was over. That was the way of mobs. Like a cresting wave, its purpose suddenly tumbled into harmless foam and formless rumbling.

Del Ordway began backing off. "We can't harm a lady, boys," he mumbled.

The tide became a turgid backwash of retreat. Ashamed now, the mob spilled out of the hotel into First Chance Gulch. There they came under the scorching eyes of Tom Chisholm who had arrived, spurring his horse.

"Go home, you idiots!" Chisholm raged. "You there, Del Ordway. You ought to know better. And you, Milt Geiger, and you . . ."

He drove them from the street like chastened children, singling them out by name. Soon the Gulch was clear with only the sheriff in sight.

Matt had watched this from the open window. He continued to stand there, facing it out to the finish. He was no murderer, and, regardless of Chisholm's plans, he refused to show anything but contempt for men who would have executed him without giving him a chance to be heard.

"Don't be foolish!" Nancy exclaimed. She seized his arm, trying to move him away from the window. "Somebody might get it in their heads to take a—"

Her fear was fulfilled. And she had probably saved his life by causing him to move. For the second time that morning a rifleshot aroused crisp echoes in the town. Matt heard the vicious sound of the bullet as it missed his head by a fraction and tore through the opposite wall.

He thrust Nancy aside and peered over the window sill. As it had been with the shot that had been meant for Tom Chisholm earlier, there was no sign of movement, no haze of powdersmoke to mark the point from which it had come.

Chisholm came bursting into the room. He looked at his daughter to make sure she was unhurt, then at Matt.

"The fellow missed again," Matt said. "He seems to be a pretty good shot, though. He doesn't miss by very much."

"Get away from that window," Chisholm snapped. "I don't want a corpse on my hands."

"You've got your daughter to thank for that," Matt said. "She's saved my bacon twice. By the way, where were you when some people came up to this room a while ago with the idea of stretching my neck?"

"I got here as soon as I could," Chisholm said. "I never was far away. How did they find out you had holed up here?"

"My fault," Matt said. "I thought I was being careful, but Paul Wallford spotted me peeking out from around the window blind. He started the ball rolling. Your daughter stopped it. She grabbed the gun from me and stood in the doorway, threatening to let daylight through some of them. She sure wilted them."

"Any idea who took that shot at you?"

Matt shrugged. "I suppose it could have been any one of half the men in town, thanks to you and your scheme, my friend. They thought mighty high of Cy Johnson. So did I. I don't know who notched on me, but, from the angle, I'd say he was shooting from inside the hayloft in that big barn at the Great Western."

The sheriff peered from the window. "Yeah!" he exclaimed, and went hurrying away.

From the window Matt watched him race away, calling other men to join him. They were heading for the big, ramshackle structure which stood on the next street and was a part of Cyrus Johnson's enterprises. It served as a warehouse and sales office for hay and grain. Its high gable roof stood above the surrounding buildings and the wide loading door of the enormous hayloft, which was empty at this early summer season, gaped down on the town and on the hotel and the street.

The sheriff returned, empty-handed. "That was the place, right enough," he said. "I could still smell the powdersmoke. But he had skedaddled. And nobody seemed to have seen hide nor hair of him. He stood well back in the hayloft, so that nobody saw the flash of the gun when he drove at you."

"The same place he stood when he ventilated your hat," Matt said. "But he wasn't aiming at your hat."

"You may be right," Chisholm said. He grinned tiredly. "Maybe we better make dust before he tries again. And also before some other people get the sand back in their craws and organize another necktie party. Both of us can't hide back of Nancy's apron. It'd be humiliating. Let's go."

"Where?"

"To jail," Chisholm said. "Where else? It's the safest place I know. We've got time to catch the morning train down to Cedar Springs. I don't think they'll try to stop us—not this soon."

"Not if your daughter goes along, at least," Matt said.

Nancy tilted up her nose. "I'm going along," she said.

An hour later the three of them were on the train, bound for the county seat. Their departure was watched sullenly but silently by the citizens of Rainbow. No hand was lifted to stop them, but it was evident that Cyrus Johnson's murder was not forgiven.

Before sundown, Matt was locked in a cell in the county jail after undergoing a long routine of booking and other legal formalities. He was charged with murder and armed robbery.

A deputy pushed him roughly into the cell. A turnkey spat scornfully on the floor as the heavy bolt was thrust in place.

"Let's have no trouble from the likes of you," the turnkey said. The man was hoping he would be given an excuse for using measures of discipline.

After they had all gone away, Matt stood

listening to the remote sounds from the sheriff's office. Tom Chisholm was seeing to it that he was spared none of the processes of law.

He became aware of the stifling limitations of the walls and bars that surrounded him. The prison smell was in his nostrils, an odor like nothing else in the world.

Proceedings were speeded against him. He was arraigned in a lower court the next day and bound over to the circuit court. A special grand jury brought an indictment of first-degree murder against him.

He went to trial two days later. The judge was Tobias Alderwood, a crusty, white-haired martinet who rushed the formalities along and would stand for no nonsense. Matt was defended by a weak attorney appointed by the court.

The trial lasted only a few hours. Paul Wallford was the principal witness. He did not look in Matt's direction as he testified that he had happened to return to the store the night of the murder and had seen Matt fleeing from the scene.

The judge's instructions to the jury were brief, but explicit. The jury remained out only long enough to eat supper at the county's expense before bringing in its verdict.

"Guilty on all counts," the jury foreman croaked. "With a recommendation that the prisoner be given a life term instead of being hung, according to the court's instructions."

"The jury is dismissed," Judge Alderwood said. He glared at Matt. "If you have anything to say, Matthew Battles, say it now. Otherwise, I am ready to pronounce sentence."

Matt shook his head. "Nothing."

"It might help you some time in the future, if and when your parole is considered, if you would restore the money you took in this crime," the judge said. "Do you know that?"

"I'll think it over," Matt said.

"You'll have plenty of time," the judge said. "I hereby sentence you to live the rest of your natural life in the state penitentiary at Stone Lodge. I remand you into custody of the sheriff who will convey you to the prison at the earliest moment."

Judge Alderwood's gavel came down. Court was dismissed. Matt looked at the handcuffs and shackles that Tom Chisholm had placed on him when he was led into court. He knew why the judge had practically forbidden the jury to return a death sentence. It was the thirty thousand dollars he was supposed to have taken. Chisholm had gotten the ear of the prosecutor and also the judge and had arranged for the life term.

Chisholm linked his own wrist to Matt's with an extra set of handcuffs. He jerked Matt roughly along and led him out of the courtroom and to a cell in the jail.

"Tough, aren't you?" Matt muttered as Chisholm freed him from the bonds and shoved him into the cell.

"Yes," Chisholm said for the benefit of the turnkey. "And I'll get tougher."

He waved the turnkey away. "I want to tell this fellow just where he stands," he explained.

To Matt, in a lower voice, he said, "We're leaving for Stone Lodge tonight. On the westbound express."

"So?"

"Do you still aim to go through with it? The plan?"

"Do you want me to quit?"

"It's up to you. You've only got a toe in the water."

"I'll keep wading," Matt said.

"It'll get deep," Chisholm said. "Plenty."

Chisholm came to the cell alone after dark and smuggled him out of the jail by a rear door. A carriage, with storm curtains buckled down, was waiting. Chisholm added a leg shackle and linked Matt's arm to a strut in the buggy's top with handcuffs.

"We've got to make this look good in case anybody sees us," he explained.

"And also to make sure I don't try to jump into a ditch and fade away," Matt said. "Why the carriage? We could have walked to the depot."

"We're going to get aboard out in the

sagebrush," Chisholm said. "Some folks pulled into town a while ago. They're from Rainbow. I got a hunch they'll be waiting somewhere around the depot. Maybe they don't figure on you leaving by train— alive at least."

"I see the point," Matt said.

Chisholm followed back streets and they emerged from town without meeting trouble. The sheriff continued to push the team. They must have covered twenty miles before reaching a flag station at a water tank along the main line of the railroad west of Cedar Springs.

The shabby house of the tank tender stood among the sagebrush. A corn patch and a hog pen flanked the shack. A milk cow sounded off mournfully in the starlight. A clothesline filled with children's garments, fluttered in the warm night breeze.

The man and his slatternly wife awakened and appeared, half-dressed. Evidently this was no uncommon event, for the man took charge of the horses and carriage without comment. "Train'll be along in about half an hour," he said. "Maw, fix the shuriff some cawfee an' flapjacks."

Matt found himself being stared at with stony blankness. Something in the expressions of the pair angered him. They gazed as though he was not human. A freak. An animal. A thing. Something beyond their understanding.

He glared back at them, mockingly. Their gaze

turned away. They were afraid of him. As afraid as they would be of a wild beast.

He saw the way Tom Chisholm watched him. He knew now what Chisholm had meant when he had talked about how deep was the water into which he was wading. For the first time, he really began to know what it meant to be looked on as beyond the pale. To be gazed at with horror and fear. To be looked on as a man who had violated the laws of decency and humanity. He was a thing that must be kept confined and only the strength of the steel fetters protected them from him. So they believed.

The woman was careful to keep the table between them when she served the food. Matt ate with one hand. The other was handcuffed to a table leg.

"What did he do?" she asked Chisholm.

"Murdered a man in a holdup," Chisholm said.

"And so young to be so vicious," the woman breathed, shuddering.

She acted as though he couldn't hear. As though he was a dumb brute. Then Matt realized it went deeper than that. She was utterly indifferent to his feelings. And so was her husband. They represented the outside world. The world of which he was no longer a part.

The westbound train presently came steaming to a halt. The fireman and water tender became busy with the spout of the tank. Heads of passengers who had been sleeping in the day cars appeared at the open windows, seeking cooler air.

Eyes gaped at Matt, handcuffed to the sheriff and hobbled by leg chains as he walked along the cinders, climbed the steps and passed down the aisles of the cars. The faces, blank and impersonal, carried the same indifference he had seen in the couple at the wayside shack. And carrying the same vague impatience as though they resented him for intruding on their complacency.

The conductor led the way to a compartment in the only Pullman on the train. The upper and lower berths were made up. The conductor too, apparently, was acquainted with the sheriff, and was repeating a familiar routine. He looked at Matt without really seeing him and said, with a laugh, "Another bird for the cage, eh, Tom?"

Chisholm locked the door after the conductor had left. The compartment was hot. He drew the blinds and freed Matt from the shackles and handcuffs. "Well?" he asked.

Matt rubbed his wrists and ankles. He rolled a cigarette. "How long will all this take?" he asked.

"No telling," Chisholm said. "Maybe a month. Maybe two, three." He added, "Maybe a year."

"A *year?*"

"This can't be rushed. You can't just walk into Stone Lodge and tell Doc Diamond you're his buddy-buddy. You've got to bait him into coming to you, to make him think you want no part of him. You've got to act like a convict, think like a convict, *be* a convict."

Matt drew on his cigarette. "That part of it won't be hard, at least. The way those people looked at me . . ."

He let the rest of it remain unsaid. He and Chisholm sat in silence, beset by the stifling heat, listening to the rumble of the train as it continued to build up speed in its rush across the vacant land.

They turned in for the night and Matt lay in the upper berth, trying to think. Rainbow seemed suddenly far, far astern and fading deeper into the mists as the train carried him onward into this new and harsh world of reality.

He thought of Mary Handley and the way she had changed from warmth to icy aloofness. In the past, he had started saving his pay, and had his eye on a small ranch in the Wind River country that might be bought at a bargain. A place for a young married couple to plant their roots. That was before the gunfight on the Sweetwater. And long, long before the train holdup. That was before his world had changed.

He told himself that this was the first step back to his old world. Someday he might be able to return to Rainbow with all the doubts and suspicions ended. To pick up where the thread had been broken, mend his life and start saving again for that small spread down in Wyoming.

He realized he was no longer able to visualize Mary Handley as a part of that plan. Yet, she was to have been the center of it. She, too, was fading into the mists.

A tightening came in his throat. He knew now that nothing would ever be the same again. In Rainbow, at least. A man could never ride over a trail in the exact footsteps of the past, no matter how hard he tried.

"There's nothing to go back to!" He hadn't meant to say it out loud. It had burst out.

Tom Chisholm surely must have heard him, but gave no sign of it. Chisholm must have understood and pitied him. That brought some of the old raging protest back in him. He wanted no pity. Not from Chisholm. Not from anyone. Not from the world. He wanted only vindication for himself and Johnny Kidd.

The train sped onward beneath the stars, stopping occasionally at way stations. The new day came and Matt had scarcely slept a wink. The sun came up. The smell of coal smoke and steam and hot leather and varnish became a part of the monotone. The heat of the long, blistering plains day increased in their small quarters. The windows rattled. Matt found himself counting the click of the rails.

Someone passed by, ringing the breakfast bell. "Meal stop in twenty minutes," the man chanted.

"Elk Bend in twenty minutes. Eatin' place in the depot."

"We could have grub brought here on trays," Chisholm said. "Or we could get off and eat in the depot. That would give us a chance to get out of this hotbox for a spell."

Matt debated it, knowing that it meant facing the stares, the blatant curiosity. But another hour of sitting here, counting the dance of the wheels, might send a man berserk. "Anything's better than this," he said.

Chisholm buckled on his gunbelt, snapped the handcuffs on Matt and picked up the leg shackles. "It'll make the other passengers easier in mind," he said.

The train ground to a stop and they emerged, joining the passengers who were pouring from the cars and hurrying into the station restaurant where the tables were already set.

The sight of handcuffs caused the space around them to clear. The food was placed on long tables, family style, but the table Chisholm chose remained vacant except for themselves.

Matt found himself responding savagely to being excommunicated from the society of his fellow men. He returned stares with stony scorn. He scowled at some of the more blatant onlookers.

Chisholm shackled him to a table leg, as usual. A waitress timorously pushed platters within reach. Matt gazed around. All the other passengers were strangers, except one. Chisholm's daughter sat two tables away, facing them.

Nancy Chisholm was eating with hearty appetite and carrying on a lively conversation with a sunbrowned, lean man whose garb was that of a prosperous rancher.

The stranger was older than she by a dozen years or more, Matt judged, but she seemed to be enjoying his attentions. She gave no sign she was aware that her father was in the eating place with a prisoner.

Matt cocked an eyebrow at Chisholm. "Sure," Chisholm muttered. "I see her. She knows it's better to stay clear of us. She got on the train at Cedar Springs. She's going to Stone Lodge with me. She's my secretary and figures she's still got to look out for me, since her mother passed away."

Matt made a second appraisal of Nancy Chisholm's companion. "That's Jeff Rossiter," Chisholm said proudly. "You've heard of the Rossiters. Flying Triangle."

"Sure," Matt said. "Big outfit."

"Biggest in these parts," Chisholm said. "Fifteen, maybe twenty thousand cattle. Gold teeth in their heads. They run a lot of stock on range along the Buffalo River west of Stone Lodge. Jeff ramrods that section of the outfit.

Him and Nancy met a couple of years ago at a stockmen's convention in Cedar Springs. He must have happened to be on the train, heading back home. He makes a lot of business trips East. I reckon Nancy will see plenty of him now that they'll be closer neighbors."

"He's old enough to be her father," Matt commented.

"Her father? What are you talking about? Jeff can't be more'n thirty-five or -six. Well, maybe forty. Nancy's no child. I'm beginning to worry about her. Can't seem to find any man that suits her. It's high time she was getting married."

" 'Specially to a rancher with gold teeth in his head. Or was it his cattle that's got 'em?"

"It's her life," Chisholm said. "I don't aim to keep her in a cage."

They quit talking. Chisholm had used the wrong word. Cage. He and Matt finished their meal in silence. The five-minute warning bell was sounding. Gulping their coffee, Chisholm freed the leg iron and they headed for their own particular cage on the train.

Matt saw Nancy Chisholm being helped aboard a car ahead by Jeff Rossiter. She was laughing gaily. Her eyes did not turn in their direction, but he had the impression her lightheartedness was a trifle forced and that she was entertaining a deep and disturbing concern for her father.

Tom Chisholm confirmed this after they were

back of a locked door again and the shackles had been removed. "Nancy didn't want me to take this warden job," he volunteered gruffly. "Every once in a while, since her mother left us, she's been after me to quit sheriffing. She wants me to go back to cattle ranching. Figures it's safer."

He was silent for a time. "Maybe I ought to have done it. For her. She worries about me. She seems to keep having dreams about me being killed."

He lighted one of his stogies and puffed savagely. "Can't blame her much. I've been shot at quite a few times. Stopped a few slugs. But I always pulled through. I guess it isn't fair to her. She's lived the biggest part of her life within sight and sound of jails. She's seen some pretty rough goings on. Life's got enough sharp edges without her having to remember things like that. Or meet people like that."

"People like me, you mean," Matt said.

Chisholm nodded. "People like you." He added, "Or at least like you're supposed to be."

"You're still not sure about me, are you?"

Chisholm cleared the ash from his smoke. "Every man has his price."

"Even you," Matt said.

"You still think I might have double-crossed you?"

"Why not?"

"All I'm here for is to help you escape with

three outlaws in the hope they'll be caught with what they stole. I won't double-cross you. But you could make a fool of me."

"So I could," Matt said. "But I couldn't turn my back on Johnny Kidd, now could I?"

"You haven't seen one hundred and twenty thousand dollars' worth of bullion bars in one pile," Chisholm said. "Gold does things to a man. It glitters."

Matt looked out at the hot flow of buffalo grass. At the summer sky. Blue, vast. "So does that," he said. "That glitters. I never want to lose that. There, a man is free."

CHAPTER SIX

They changed trains, shifting to a branch line and rode in a day coach where Matt was continually pinned down by staring eyes. Matt discovered that Nancy Chisholm was still aboard, and still accompanied by Jeff Rossiter.

It was nearing midnight when they alighted at last at the small, dingy depot at Stone Lodge. Mountain ridges stood up against the stars. The dank smell of the river mingled with that of sagebrush and pines, for Stone Lodge stood on the south bank of a tributary to the Missouri. The prison crouched, black and forbidding, on a hill that dominated the town and overlooked the stream.

The midnight wind, still hot, kicked up dust in the silent unpaved street. A prison wagon—a plank box on wheels, with a padlocked door and tiny, barred slits for air—stood waiting. Two prison guards loomed in the light of the oil lamp that hung over the station door. They were burly men, carrying pistols, with long clubs in the belts of their faded blue uniforms. One had a bull's-eye lantern with which he promptly blinded Matt.

They seized Matt's arms with rough, powerful hands. "We'll take care of this one," the bigger of the two said in a heavy voice. "You're Chisholm, the new warden, ain't you? I'm Ed Ledge, captain o' guards."

Chisholm shook hands perfunctorily with Ed Ledge. The other guard said, "I'm Pete Coulter. I see you brung us a new bird for the cage. What's his name?"

"Battles," Chisholm said. "Life term for killing in an armed robbery."

"I recollect hearin' about this fellow," Ed Ledge said. "It was in the newspaper here. Knife killin' at Rainbow, wasn't it? Unarmed man he rubbed out. Stole quite a chunk of money, as I recall it. Thirty thousand dollars."

Matt felt Ledge's beefy hand close tighter on his arm. Ledge had great strength and evidently gloried in using it.

"We don't like knife men here at Stone Lodge," Ledge said. "You stabbed this fella in the back, didn't you?"

"Not with a knife," Matt said. "I ran a spike of a miner's candlestick in him, so they told the jury."

"Boastin' about it, are you," Coulter snarled. He jammed the knuckles of his clenched fist against Matt's jaw and shoved him off balance. "Well, we take the temper out'n that kind here on the Hill."

Tom Chisholm watched this in silence. "I'll take care of booking him after I get straightened out on the job, tomorrow," he said. "I'll turn him

106

over to you now, Ledge. Take no chances with him. He's rough. My daughter was on the train and is waiting for me."

"There's a carriage here fer you an' the girl, Chisholm," Ledge said. "Like you asked in your telegram." He pointed. "That's it tied up at the end o' the depot."

"From now on, Ledge," Chisholm said, "when you address me, my title is warden or sir. Or Mr. Chisholm."

Ledge, scowling, saluted elaborately. "Yes, sir!" he said jeeringly.

Chisholm removed the cuffs that linked his wrist with Matt's. "Follow orders, Battles," he said. "Keep in line. Toe the chalk."

"Yes, sir!" Matt said mockingly.

"A prison is what a man makes it," Chisholm said. "It can be an atonement, a cleansing of the soul, or it can be a hell on earth. It's up to you."

He added, "Good night, Ledge. Good night, Coulter."

He walked away. Matt saw that Nancy Chisholm had alighted from the train, along with Jeff Rossiter, and was waiting. Her father joined them, and they moved to where a carriage was waiting and there Rossiter parted from them.

Ledge shoved Matt toward the prison van. "So it's warden, or sir, or mister, is it!" he snarled to Coulter. "It seems like we've got one o' the spit an' polish kind to sit in the front office. He'll learn who runs the Hill. Learn the hard way. It is myself that will teach him."

"The hard way," Coulter echoed.

Together they sent Matt plunging headlong into the prison van. With his hands linked at his back, he was unable to protect himself. He twisted as he fell, taking the weight of his fall on his shoulder. Coulter kicked him on the thigh, then slammed the door, locking him in the van.

Up to this moment he had kept telling himself that it was all a pretense and that everything would be straightened out in time by Tom Chisholm. Even the killing of Cyrus Johnson would be explained and the guilty one found.

For the first time, he knew sickening doubt—and terror. He became aware of his helplessness. Shackled and dominated by brutalized men like Ledge and Coulter. At the mercy of them and perhaps other sadistic prison guards. Facing weeks and months, perhaps, of association with felons whose crimes were real.

What if it stretched out for a year? For years? For life? What if Tom Chisholm became convinced he really had murdered Cyrus Johnson? What if Chisholm was the real killer after all?

The prison van rattled on its way through the silent streets of the town. He managed to wriggle his way to his knees and to one of the plank seats. He braced himself there.

Presently, his head lifted. An odor with which

he had grown familiar in the Cedar Springs jail became all too evident. The musty, sickly sweet blend of whitewashed walls, of lime, of confined humans, of sweat and sorrow, of leather brogans and the rough cotton from which prison stripes are woven. Of damp walls, of monotony and despair. This was the prison smell. Different from Cedar Springs. Deeper, unforgettable. Terrifying.

He heard an iron gate creak, heard the banter of rough voices as the gatekeeper let the wagon enter. The jolting ended and the door of the van was opened.

"Come out o' there, you!" Ledge commanded. "An' in a hell of a hurry!"

Ledge reached inside the van, knocked off Matt's hat and seized his hair, dragging him down the steps of the vehicle to the ground. Matt twisted around, got to his knees and managed to whirl so that both of his manacled hands drove into the pit of Ledge's stomach.

Ledge reeled back with a moan of agony. Coulter uttered profanity. "Why, you damned scum!" He leaped at Matt, kicking out with a heavy shoe. The brogan caught Matt in the side and he felt a shock of pain. Coulter kicked again.

This time Matt was ready for him. He partly evaded the shoe, but let it slip beneath his armpit and then clamped his arm around the guard's leg. He whirled and sent Coulter crashing backward against a stone wall.

For a moment he had a respite. Ledge had not yet recovered his breath and Coulter was too shaken by the force of his fall. But he saw that he was eventually going to pay for his resistance. Pay in pain.

"All right!" Ledge panted. "So you hang tough!"

Overhead loomed the lonely jewels that were stars. They glittered above the dark, brooding mass of the prison walls and the flat tops of the cell blocks. Above the jagged rims of the silent mountains.

Around them and close at hand were other shadows, and the shapes of cell doors. At those doors were faces. Staring faces. Silent faces. Caged men. This was the heart of Stone Lodge, the prison on the hill above the foaming Buffalo River. The convicts had awakened and were watching the baptism of a new companion in this world of the lost.

Matt saw the dark, ugly swing of the clubs in the hands of Ledge and Coulter. One of these weapons caught him on the arm. More pain drove through him. A second thudded on his left thigh and he staggered, his leg numb.

The clubs were flat and hard-padded, with coverings of soft leather so that they would not cut the skin. They were weighted so that each blow had bruising power.

Matt twisted and ducked, diving at them, trying to use his head as a ram. Trying to kick at them, trying with what poor weapons he had, not only to defend himself, but to give them blow for blow.

It was hopeless. They circled, keeping him between them, and the clubs kept landing with harsh, agonizing force. He realized they intended to beat him until he groveled for mercy.

He was aware of the silence, except for the soft sound of the clubs. Of the impersonal, stony silence of those faces at the cell doors. As impersonal as the stars above, as indifferent to the brutality of the guards and the punishment he was taking as the massive walls that confined them.

He became aware that Tom Chisholm had returned and was watching his ordeal. The warden stood a few paces back and was making no attempt to intercede in the unequal contest.

A club landed across Matt's stomach, driving the breath from him. He dizzily realized that there was another spectator. The big, main gates were still open. The broad landscaped area in front of the prison was lighted by acetylene lamps on the walls.

The carriage in which Chisholm had arrived stood in front of a square, red brick residence which adjoined and seemed even a part of the prison. This evidently served as office and residence for the warden.

Nancy Chisholm had alighted from the carriage,

a traveling case in her hand. She was standing, staring at the scene in the prison yard. Like her father, she was making no sign of protest or even of pity.

A club felled Matt. Another blow completed the job. He lay stretched out, unable to continue the fight.

Ledge shoved a shoe roughly into his ribs. "Get up!"

It was minutes before Matt could drag himself to his knees, then to his feet. He expected the clubbing to start again.

But Tom Chisholm spoke. "That ought to be lesson enough, for this time. Put him in a cell until I have time to hear his case, Mr. Ledge."

He addressed Matt. "As for you, let me warn you that disobedience is a serious offense. I'll teach you not to lay hands on a guard. You'll do dungeon time for this."

Chisholm strode away through the gate and joined his daughter at the door of the residence. The heavy gate swung closed and bars slid into place. Armed guards on the walls, who had converged at that point, ready for trouble, scattered back to their posts elsewhere. Matt saw the nose of a Gatling gun bristling from a tower that stood higher than all the walls.

"Get movin'," Ledge said and shoved him ahead.

He was prodded past the line of silent faces

toward a barred door that Ledge opened. Inside was darkness. Not the darkness of the starlit night. The darkness of a cave. Matt realized that the barred door was actually set into the face of living rock.

He was pushed into this darkness. The beam of the bull's-eye lantern in Coulter's hands seemed to recoil from the blackness. It touched on rough-carved rock walls and on cell doors set into the granite hill. Faces, gray and pasty, appeared briefly in the moving beam, then were a part of the darkness. He was pushed into a cell. The door closed with a groan of metal and the grating of the bolts.

Footsteps retreated. The bull's-eye vanished and the outer door clanged shut. A jeering voice spoke from somewhere nearby in the darkness. "Welcome to Dungeon Block. Who are you, and what was your sin?"

Matt said, "That's for me to know."

The voice laughed. "We'll all know soon enough. There're no secrets in hell. And this is where the devil lives. You're almost at the bottom of the pit."

Another voice spoke. A cultured voice, but it carried the keen, cruel edge of honed steel. "No more talk! Be quiet, so I can sleep!"

The first speaker's tone changed, becoming suddenly very respectful. "I didn't mean anything, Mr. Diamond."

Silence came. Matt waited, listening. Around him he knew that the inmates of Dungeon Block were going back to sleep. But he had many things to think about. And one of these was that he had heard the voice of the man who was the reason for his being here. Doc Diamond's voice had been that of authority among these souls in purgatory.

He moved in the darkness—and collided with stone. He turned in another direction. Stone again. Probing with his hands, he found the rough frame of a bunk which occupied nearly the length of his tomb. It had a thin mattress.

By stretching his arms he could touch the walls on either side. As his eyes became tuned to the darkness, he discovered that he could make out the outline of a small opening in the solid iron door of his cell. This admitted an elusive luminescence that filtered in from the bigger main door to the cell room. Starlight. The light of the great, free spaces that he had known all his life.

Panic came. He was breathing hard and fast. Again the cultured voice spoke nearby. "Easy, my friend. Easy! There's always an end to every pain. An answer to every prayer."

Doc Diamond's voice softened to a mere echo. "There are even ways out of hell."

"I'm listening," Matt whispered.

There was no answer. All Matt could hear

was the breathing of the other prisoners. That seemed to merge into a single, throbbing pulse. A rhythmic dirge. The pulse of the prison. Its voice.

Matt found himself shaking with fever as an aftermath of his battle with the guards. His body ached from the beating. He did not sleep that night, although the worse effects of the clubbing wore off, leaving only the memory of the brutality.

CHAPTER SEVEN

Matt was marched out at sunrise to the supply room where he was issued a striped uniform of coarse, wrinkled cotton cloth, along with heavy cowhide shoes and a few other necessities. His own clothing was taken away. Next, his hair was close-clipped by a prison barber.

Along with other convicts, he marched, lockstep, to the mess hall for breakfast. No talk was allowed. One convict, a wild-eyed man with sunken eyes, whispered something to a neighbor. He was snatched from the table by two guards, rapped across the back of his thighs with billies and hustled away, foodless.

Matt scanned the faces of the others at his table. Some had their legs shackled to ringbolts beneath the benches. Brutal faces were in the majority. He realized that this table was exclusively for inmates of Dungeon Block, and that these were the incorrigibles, the worst of the felons in the prison. He and his companions were watched closely by guards who held shotguns cocked and at the ready.

Ed Ledge came into the long room, wearing his captain's uniform. He singled out Matt, strode to the table and, without warning, tried to push Matt's face down into his bowl of cornmeal mush. Matt had guessed what was coming and had braced himself.

Ledge, powerful as he was, and not expecting resistance, failed to more than budge Matt's head. Ledge was the one who suffered defeat. His discomfiture brought silent, gleeful derision into the faces of the other convicts.

Ledge was furious, but he decided against risking another setback in the presence of the incorrigibles. "You'll soften, you scum!" he said. "Soften to putty. I'll see to that!" He turned and strode scowling out of the mess hall.

Matt marked one of the Dungeon Block squad as far different from the common run. This convict was tall, well-proportioned so that he looked slender. He had left one space between himself and the men on either side when he had taken his place at the table, thereby setting himself apart. The guards had not objected to this procedure. Here was a felon who was either being accorded special privilege or was being given particular surveillance.

This man, Matt surmised, was Doc Diamond, the possessor of the icy, cultured voice. For once, here was a person whose appearance and manners were in keeping with his reputation as a fastidious gentleman, bandit, gambler, black-sheep aristocrat—and killer.

Even in stripes and with hair cut short he was handsome in a metallic way. He had eyes that were very dark and very intelligent, but with no warmth. His nose was thin and predatory. His mouth and jaw line were sharp-cut. He seemed to be in his early forties.

Diamond ate leisurely. It was evident he scorned those felons who were wolfing their food like animals. He glanced once in Matt's direction. Matt felt that he was being keenly appraised.

In turn, he studied Diamond whenever the man's attention was elsewhere. He was remembering stories he had heard about the gambler. Stories of miraculous surgical feats the man had performed—of babies and mothers saved in childbirth, of operations on wounded men on saloon pool tables or in mine shafts.

And other stories of callous indifference when Diamond, for no apparent reason, had refused to turn a hand to help persons in circumstances similar to the other cases. He was a man of moods, of dramatic heights, and of black depths. Above all, he was lawless.

Matt studied the others at the table, wondering if the two men Tom Chisholm had named as having been in on the train robbery with Diamond, were among the dungeon group.

From a description Chisholm had given him during the train trip, he believed that one convict at the table might be Turk Shagrue. This man sat almost opposite him and was of a different stripe from the velvet-mannered Diamond. He was blocky of body, slope-shouldered with a broken nose and a face scarred by violence. If this was really Turk Shagrue, he had the manners of a pig. He ate noisily and was intent only on satisfying his hunger.

If Frank Welton was present, Matt could not identify him from Chisholm's description.

The meal ended and orders were barked. Matt found that Doc Diamond was directly back of him as they marched back to their cells.

"You handle Ledge wrong," Diamond murmured. "You're only giving him the excuse to muss you up. He loves that sort of thing. Don't buck him—openly. It doesn't pay."

"I've got no use for him, or his kind," Matt growled.

"I'm giving you good advice, Battles," Diamond said.

"So you know my name?"

"Of course. You're in for killing a man in a—"

A guard lunged at them, a club lifted. "No talking in ranks, you two!"

He looked at Diamond. He said nothing more, but backed away to his former distance. Matt marched onward in the bitter lockstep. But he had learned one thing: the guards were afraid of Doc Diamond.

Matt was locked in the dungeon-like cell and was brought out only at evening mealtime to march again to the mess hall. The incorrigibles were fed only twice a day. During their sessions in the eating hall every guard in the prison went on the alert, heavily armed.

He learned also that Dungeon Block was not considered a dungeon, either by the other convicts or the guards. Evidently there was another, blacker dungeon in this place.

News was passed along by way of a system that was a blend of significant looks, facial expressions and, especially, finger talk. The inmates of Stone Lodge had their own sign language. He was to discover that it could be very eloquent, very informative.

A full day passed. He paced his cell, torn by alternate bursts of helpless fury and intervals of doubt and apprehension. Why had not Chisholm communicated with him? Was the warden abandoning him, leaving him to serve out his life for a crime he had not committed?

The heat of the plains summer beat down on the outer prison, but the cells of the incorrigibles escaped the worst of this, insulated by the mass of living rock. Even so, there was a breathless, suffocating sensation. It was like being trapped in a cavern with volcanic fires close at hand.

Their marches to the mess hall for supper gave Matt a taste of what the Hill really had to offer. This journey carried them across the long expanse of open prison yard whose clay surface had been exposed all day to the sun.

With the walls of the cell blocks reflecting the glare, it was a fiery gantlet. The surface burned even through the heavy soles of Matt's shoes. The shade of the mess hall doorway seemed like a haven, although the room itself was torrid with the heat of the nearby kitchen ovens and the laundry boilers.

Darkness of another day came. And no word from Chisholm. Except for the few whispers he had traded with Doc Diamond on the first day, he had not spoken to anyone since being issued his stripes and a number.

He lay on the hard bunk, a caged animal that had given up its freedom. A freedom he wanted back. From that instant all his thoughts, all his waking moments, even his dreams were occupied with one intention. Escape!

It was the afternoon of the fourth day when Ledge and Coulter came tramping to his cell and unbarred the door. "Out!" Ledge commanded. "Lively! Double time!"

Prodding him with their clubs, they marched him across the blazing prison yard to a small iron door that opened into the comparative coolness of a carpeted hallway. Matt saw that they had entered the adjoining building which housed the office and home of the warden.

"It's about time," he said.

Ledge rapped him across the back of his thighs with the club—a favorite manner of punishment on the part of the guards. The blow dealt sharp, torturing pain. It could paralyze the muscles for a time. Or permanently, if delivered with strength.

They moved down the hall to the glass-paneled door of the warden's office. It was Nancy Chisholm who opened the door when Ledge knocked. She wore a severely plain white blouse and dark skirt, and had dark sleeve protectors to her elbows. A pencil was thrust in her hair. A desk was stacked with files and papers.

"Come in," she said. "The warden is ready to see this man."

She ushered them to the open door of an inner office. Tom Chisholm sat at a desk that was equally heavy with documents. He bore the harassed look of a man swamped by paper work.

"Come in," he said. His eyes were hard, impersonal as he pushed aside a document and gazed at Matt. "Oh, yes, Battles. I want to talk to you."

"Convict No. 1571," Ledge corrected. "We don't call 'em by name here on the Hill."

Chisholm gave Ledge a slanting, critical look. He fished through a file of papers and brought a memorandum to light.

"You're charged with assault on the guards and insubordination," he said.

Matt bristled. He had expected something more than this. Chisholm could hardly be anything but formal and official in the presence of Ledge, but he could at least have given some hint that this was not exactly a routine procedure. A look, a lowering of an eyelid. But there was nothing. All of Matt's doubts flared into new life.

"Not guilty!" he snapped.

"You've already been found guilty," Chisholm said harshly. "I witnessed the affair with my own eyes."

He added curtly, "Ten days in the dungeon on bread and water."

Ledge spoke angrily. "Only ten days? He ought to git thirty. He tried to kill me an' Coulter. He's got to be taught—"

"I'm taking into account the fact he is a newcomer," Chisholm said. "I'll deal with him with sharper spurs if he gets out of line again."

He added, "That'll be all. I'm very busy. Take him away." Chisholm had already returned to his problems with the paper work. At her desk, Nancy Chisholm finished taking notes of the conversation. She opened a ledger and picked up a pen, evidently to enter the matter formally in the prison records.

Ledge pushed Matt toward the outer door of the office. Matt resisted. He was aghast at the severity of the sentence, but, above all, by its utter impersonality. Nancy Chisholm's eyes lifted for an instant but passed over him, then returned to her task. She, too, treated him as only a number and not a human being.

He was marched back across the torrid prison yard. But he was not taken back to the cell he had occupied. He was prodded to another iron door, set deeper in bedrock. Ledge opened this door and Coulter came with a bull's-eye. Matt was pushed inside.

"Have fun in the snake pit," Ledge said.

The door closed. All light vanished. Matt waited, expecting his eyes to tell him something when they became tuned to the gloom. Nothing happened. Nothing.

This was the real dungeon. This was the snake pit. Lightless. Completely. Soundless as far as the outside world was concerned. All he could hear were the scraping movements of his shoes on stone. Even this seemed to be swallowed instantly by the blackness around him.

He moved around, exploring with arms outstretched. He stumbled over a metal object. It was a sizable iron ring set in the stone floor. There were other rings. Half a dozen in all.

He felt along the walls, moving slowly. Always his search brought him back to the small iron door. This was the only opening. He paced off the length and width of the place. Eight steps in one direction, eight in another. He could touch the rock ceiling with his hands.

He shouted loudly, frantically. The walls did not even send back an echo. He stood, muscles contorted, fists clenched, hating Tom Chisholm, hating Ledge, hating the world. He was sure now that Chisholm had betrayed him.

Chisholm had said that life in this place could seem to last a thousand years. Matt learned the truth. The bread that he ate each day was dry and crusty. The water tasted of alkali. The twenty-minute reprieve each morning, when he was allowed to emerge from the dungeon for exercise and to wash and shave, began to be the only moments he was alive. The remainder of the twenty-four hours was a form of death.

It was on the third day of his confinement that he had a visitor. The door was unbolted and swung open. He was blinded by the beam of a bull's-eye.

Ledge's voice spoke. "All right, Warden. You there, 1571, mind your manners. An' stand to attention. The warden wants to talk to you."

Tom Chisholm's voice spoke. "Close the door, Ledge. I want to talk to this man alone. He needs some good advice."

"This here fella is tough," Ledge objected. "He—"

"I'm armed," Chisholm said impatiently. "I can take care of myself. You can leave now."

The lantern changed hands. Matt saw Ledge departing. The door clanged shut. Chisholm swung the beam around the dungeon. For the first time Matt actually saw the rock walls. Up to that moment they had been rough surfaces

126

without character, without reality. Now he stood in the presence of impenetrable granite. The drill holes for the powder that had been used to blast out this cave showed here and there.

The beam paused on him, dazzling him again, and he backed away. "Damn you," he said to Chisholm.

The beam lowered to the floor. "Don't be a fool, Battles," Chisholm said loudly so that his voice could be heard beyond the dungeon door. "You can make it easier on yourself, or you can spend your life in the snake pit. It's up to you. That's what I came to talk to you about."

Matt heard faint sounds of footsteps receding beyond the door.

Chisholm stood listening a moment until satisfied Ledge was not eavesdropping. His voice lowered and changed. "How are you making out, Battles?"

Matt didn't reply for a moment. Hope suddenly returned. "I'll make out," he said cautiously. "In spite of everything. In spite of you. In spite of hell."

"I know what you're thinking," Chisholm said. "But it has to be done this way. I couldn't handle it any other way. Particularly in front of Ledge. He's watching me, waiting for mistakes. He'd jump at anything he saw out of line and become suspicious. He might talk if he guessed what we

127

had in mind. It would get to Diamond. Then how long do you think you'd last?"

"You tell me," Matt said.

"Maybe a day. Maybe a week if you're lucky. I've already made one mistake. I should have given you at least twenty days in the snake pit. To satisfy Ledge, if nothing else. That's the minimum jolt for hitting a guard. It's usually thirty days."

"Thirty? A man would go loco."

"If it comes that way, I'll send you here for thirty days," Chisholm said. "And you won't go loco. You've got a job to do. You can't afford to."

"And why not?"

"Not if you want to help out Johnny Kidd. Not if you want to convince me you didn't kill Cy Johnson. Not if you want to live. Maybe you still don't know the kind of snakes you're playing with. A man like Doc Diamond—"

"I've met Diamond," Matt said.

"You have? You mean you've talked to him already?"

"Only a few words. But I can tell you one thing. He's going to try to bust out of this place."

"Of course!" Chisholm snapped. "That's taken for granted. Half the men in here have the same thing in mind. But, my God man, you haven't made the mistake of working too fast, I hope! Diamond will smell a trap, get suspicious you were planted."

"No. He did all the talking, not me."

"Likely he put the acid on you, trying to assay you."

"Sure. That's what I'd do if I was doing his thinking."

"Good," Chisholm said.

"What do you mean—good?"

"You're beginning to think like a convict. Act like one."

"I've got good reason. You know what I mean. You're the only man who knows the real reason I went into Cy Johnson's mercantile. The only one who could tell the truth and get me out of this place. *If* you want to tell it."

"You still think I might be the one who killed Cy and took that money, don't you?" Chisholm said incredulously.

"I've only got your word that you didn't."

"But I've told you there is one other party who knows all about that holdup," said Chisholm.

"I remember. But you haven't mentioned who it is."

"I told you it'd be best if you didn't know, but that you could trust this person to the finish."

"That's for me to judge," Matt said. "But, to tell the truth, I believe I already know who this person is."

Chisholm peered at him, then shrugged. "I see that you've guessed it. You're right. It's my daughter, Nancy."

"That was a stupid thing to do. You know that."

"She's the one I'm absolutely sure I could trust. The only one in this world."

"Why are you so sure? Women are gossips."

"You can bet your neck on this particular woman."

"That's what I'm doing," Matt said. "My neck. Not yours."

"I've got to leave now," Chisholm said. "I'm afraid I've dallied too long here already. I'm going to visit other tough convicts. I can't afford to let Ledge think I'm favoring you."

"It hasn't looked that way up to now."

"I'll bear down even harder on you if need be."

"All I ask," Matt said, "is that you keep Ledge off my back."

"Ledge is your problem. He runs the cell blocks. I can't give you any help in that direction."

"Maybe you really don't want to give me any help."

Chisholm refused to debate that. "You're going to have company soon," he said. "Doc Diamond."

"Diamond? Here? You're going to dungeon him?"

"I'm giving him ten days in the pit. A meat cleaver was missing from the kitchen today. Diamond was seen in the kitchen this morning. He had no business there."

"Did you find the cleaver?"

"No. Diamond's too smart for that. Other things

have vanished lately. A hoe and the blade of a scythe from the tools the trusties use down on the garden patch by the river. And other items."

"Where would a man hide stuff like that in this place? It's like trying to hide a wart on your nose."

"I wish I knew. Ledge tells me he's turned this prison upside-down and hasn't found a trace of anything that would help us."

"What about your stool pigeons? Can't they help you?"

"Not where Diamond is concerned. The pigeons all lost their wings after the one I told you about was rubbed out. They're strictly scared."

"You hope I might be luckier."

"You'll get a chance to become better acquainted with Diamond. You'll be birds of a feather here in solitary."

With that, Chisholm went to the door, pounded on the iron with the handle of a six-shooter until Ledge let him out, and left without another word.

Darkness clamped down again on Matt. Presently the door opened once more. Guards entered with their blinding lanterns. Shackles clanked. Matt was shoved against a wall and an ankle was shackled to one of the rings embedded in the floor.

Another convict was being shackled to another ring. The lantern beam passed over the thin face of Doc Diamond. He wore a scornful, bitter smile.

"Maybe you'll now have a chance to think and recall where you hid that cleaver, Diamond," Tom Chisholm said.

Diamond laughed. "Do me a favor, Warden. Just hold your breath until I do remember. In fact, I'd like nothing better than to hold it for you. Permanently."

"I'm sure you would," Chisholm said.

"Maybe I'll be lucky some other time," Diamond said.

The guards and Chisholm left. The door was bolted. For a time there was only the sound of Matt's pulse in his ears. He tested his shackle and found that the heavy chain that linked him to the iron ring was less than two feet long. He could take only one short step in any direction. He stretched his arms, but could not reach the walls.

Diamond spoke. "Battles?"

"That's me," Matt growled surlily. "Who'd you think it was. Santa Claus? These aren't bells I'm jingling."

Diamond chuckled. "Take it easy, cowboy. You *are* a cowboy, aren't you? You talk like a man who's jingled spur chains instead of leg irons all your life."

"I *was* a cowboy," Matt said.

"And now you're a number like the rest of us."

"My name's Battles. Matt Battles."

"Not to Chisholm. Not to anybody but yourself."

"If you've got nothing better to say, then don't say anything," Matt snarled.

Diamond laughed again, pleased. "Do you know who I am?"

"No," Matt said. "And don't bother telling me. I don't give a hoot."

"My name's Diamond. They call me Doc Diamond." Diamond paused, waiting expectantly. When Matt didn't answer, he added, somewhat miffed. "You've heard of me, of course?"

"Seems like I have," Matt said. "You're a tinhorn, as I recall it."

Diamond's vanity was hurt. He was angrily silent for a time. But that passed. He laughed again. "Never mind. You'll learn."

They quit talking. Together, they endured the endless tedium. Endured the stillness, the timelessness. The only breaks were the rest periods in the mornings when they were marched to the wash rooms, and the moments, morning and evening, when they were given bread and water.

At times they paced the halting circles around the clanking rings that held them. Mainly, they stretched out on the stone floor and forced themselves to enter a mental coma that was their only armor against insanity.

At times they talked aimlessly, listlessly. Talk

133

that did not touch on themselves and what was uppermost in Matt's mind. Small talk. Diamond's special subject was an endless repertoire of stories of high-play gambling, in which he displayed incredible skill and always emerged the winner of big pots. At other times he talked of gunfights and of his speed and marksmanship.

Some of these tales, no doubt, were based on fact, but mainly the stories were fanciful and were intended only to impress Matt and build an image of Diamond's invincibility.

Deep-down, Diamond really believed these things and their telling fed his self-esteem. But the man had another purpose in mind and Matt realized this just in time. Almost in self-defense he longed to relate some of the high spots of his own life. Such as the time he and Johnny the Kid had faced heavy odds through gunsmoke and had come out of it alive. Then there had been moments of glory when he and Johnny had split up the day money at the Cheyenne and Bozeman rodeos. There was the day at Pendleton when he had ridden out Red Furnace, a horse that no buckaroo had been able to stay with to the whistle.

He resisted the impulse to strut a little. He let Diamond do the talking. His hunch had been right. On the last day of his term in the dungeon, Diamond said, "I'm beginning to cotton to you. I like a man who knows enough to keep his mouth shut. You haven't told me a thing about yourself."

"I can't say the same about you," Matt said.

Diamond chuckled. "Never mind, Battles, if that is your real name."

Matt understood that he had passed some kind of a test. Diamond had shed his talkative, self-glorification role. He was tacitly conceding that it had been a trap to draw Matt out. And he had failed.

Matt's respect for the man's shrewdness increased. It was plain that the slightest slip would be fatal.

Diamond finally put it into words. "What would you give to get out of this place, Battles?"

"Two bits," Matt said. After a long time, he added, "A leg maybe. My best girl. My chance of heaven."

Diamond gave a sniff. "The world's full of arms and girls and the chance at heaven. Try pawning things like that for cash money."

"What do you know about heaven?"

"Only that there're no pockets in a shroud. Or in wings. It's only cash that counts in this world."

"I'm listening," Matt said.

"Money talks. Even in Stone Lodge. Above all, in Stone Lodge."

"So money talks. There are no pockets in a suit of stripes either."

"I'm not talking about chickenfeed. Just to say something, say you could lay your hands on some thick cash if somebody helped you get out of here. What would it be worth to you?"

"Just to say something, Diamond, let's get down to cases. How much?"

Diamond laughed. "Hell, Battles, we know that the only reason they didn't hang you for killing that store owner in Rainbow is that they know you've got thirty thousand dollars hid out somewhere in the sagebrush."

"So I'm rich out in the sagebrush," Matt said. "But I'm in Stone Lodge."

"Do you want to get out of here or not?"

"Do you mean you want to deal me in on my own money?" Matt asked scornfully. "I pay the freight for you? Now let me laugh for a while."

Diamond lost his icy calm. "I can top any chip you shove in," he said. "I'll match you, dollar for dollar, on what it takes to get out of here. I've got two men who'll stick with me. I've decided you might stack up."

"You interest me," Matt said. "Up to a point. But this is too sudden. Maybe you're just setting me up, so that you can squeal on me so as to get in soft with Chisholm."

Diamond burst into scornful laughter. "Me? Doc Diamond trying to toady to a warden? You're loco."

The footsteps of guards sounded, approaching the door of the dungeon. "Talk fast," Matt said. "I think I'm about to leave this cozy little place.

Unless I'm wrong, this is the end of my ten-day rest cure."

"I'll get in touch with you at the right time," Diamond said.

The dungeon door opened. The bull's-eye lantern hurt Matt's eyes again. "All right, you!" Ledge's voice growled. "It's my guess you'll be back in the pit before the week's out."

He was marched into the open prison yard. It was nearing sundown and his eyes could not endure the blazing sunlight after ten days of its absence. He stood breathless and panting in the heat.

Ledge's beefy hand slapped hard against his back, sending him staggering ahead. "Move on, you scum!"

He was locked in his original cell in Dungeon Block, but here, at least, was light. Faint, but tangible. It came from the sun. And from the open sky. The great open sky under which he might ride again. The free sky.

For Doc Diamond had as much as admitted that he had access to money if he escaped from Stone Lodge. A lot of money.

Matt thought of Johnny Kidd. And of the post card he had received. There his thinking stopped.

He awakened in the morning, buoyed by a high excitement. He scanned the faces of the convicts around him as he marched to the mess hall. He didn't know exactly what he expected to find, but Diamond's veiled remark indicated that a big break was being hatched.

What he found was nothing. Absolutely nothing in the stolid faces around him. Prison faces. Resigned faces. Blank faces. The living dead. Their lives had ended and only their bodies had animation. These were the lifers. Murderers. Their only thankfulness was that they had escaped the gallows.

He realized that he was regarded as one of these faceless men. Whenever the eyes of other convicts met his gaze it was as though they didn't see him. It came to him that he had been written off as a person, not only by the outer world but by the living dead around him. He was nothing. Without a future, paying for the past.

His expectancy faded as the days passed. Nothing happened. Each day was a duplicate of its predecessor, a forecast of the one to follow. The segment of the great sky above the open prison yard also became like a barrier of hot blue steel. Occasionally thunderstorms cooled the prison, but mainly there was no respite during the torrid days or the long, hot nights when he lay, listening to the moans and cries and heavy breathing of other denizens of the cages.

CHAPTER EIGHT

Doc Diamond had served his time in the dungeon and had resumed his place in the lockstep marches, eating the rough prison fare in scornful silence. He seemed to go out of his way to avoid Matt and never glanced in his direction.

Matt had identified both of Diamond's partners in the stage holdup, for which they had been sentenced. He had been correct in assuming that the flat-nosed, hard-eyed man who sat opposite him in the mess hall at each meal was Turk Shagrue.

Frank Welton, the third of the trio, was not quartered in Dungeon Block, but marched with the lesser strata of felons. At first Matt believed this was because Welton was not looked on as being as dangerous as the other two. He came to revise that opinion. Welton, at first glance, appeared to be only a reckless, handsome, thoughtless man who had been led astray by others. He might have served as a model for a Remington or a Russell. That was until Matt was able to study the man. Welton's pale eyes held no compassion. He was feared by the other convicts. The real reason he was not held in Dungeon Block was that the guards wanted the trio kept separated.

Although Diamond continued to pointedly avoid any contact, Matt realized that he was being studied and appraised by Welton and Turk Shagrue. That kept an ember of hope alive in him.

On two occasions, while wielding a broom with the cleanup squad in the prison yard, he saw Nancy Chisholm. It was sundown each time, and also each time she was joining Jeff Rossiter, who was waiting with a flashy palomino for himself and another bearing a sidesaddle. Jeff Rossiter's courtship was persistent.

If Nancy Chisholm was aware that he was one of the stripe-wearing convicts, she gave no sign of it and never glanced into the prison yard. She was always gay and smiling as she rode away at Rossiter's side.

He began to resent Nancy Chisholm's indifference to his plight. And he envied Rossiter almost to the point of detesting him. But it was Ed Ledge he came to loathe completely.

The captain of guards returned that dislike and went out of his way to demonstrate it. Matt was disciplined often for petty infractions of the rules, some of which were imaginary. He served long hours in the kitchens where the cookstoves made existence almost unbearable, or in the laundry, working on the steaming vats.

He again began to believe that he was being betrayed by Tom Chisholm. He had not even glimpsed the warden in nearly a month. In desperation, one morning, he hurled his plate of food against a wall in the mess hall.

Guards rushed up, their clubs raised, and dragged him out of the place. Ledge was called. He arrived, grinning.

"So you don't like what we feed you," he said. "Maybe a little session in the sun will change your mind. Let him fry at the whipping post for a while."

The whipping post stood in the center of the prison yard, but it was no longer used for its original purpose. Tom Chisholm had ordered an end to that form of punishment.

Ledge had found other use for the post. Matt was marched into the yard and shackled to the post. "You'll wait here until I find time to take you to the warden," Ledge said. "It'll be the dungeon again for you, tough guy."

Ledge stripped the striped shirt from him, leaving him bare to the waist in the blazing sun.

"You need to be tanned up a little," Ledge grinned. "You got a nice pink skin for a growed man."

Matt's face and hands and forearms were impervious to the sun, tanned almost saddle color. But not his body. He knew what he was in for. Half an hour in the sun, and it would be as agonizing as though Ledge had poured scalding water on his back. He had heard stories of convicts moaning and raving in delirium after Ledge's sun treatments.

He tried to circle the post so that even its meager shadow would give him some protection. But he could feel the power of the sun on his skin.

Ledge stood watching, chuckling. "Stake him so he can't wriggle around, Pete," he said to Coulter.

Sharp steps sounded in the prison yard. And the flutter of skirts. Nancy Chisholm had appeared from the warden's quarters and was approaching, walking fast. Her eyes were flashing angrily. She was ignoring a strict prison rule that forbade the appearance of any of her sex inside the prison proper.

Her arrival on forbidden ground shattered the lifeless crust of the prison, revealing the fires beneath. Convicts in the cell blocks aroused. A low, animal-like rumble arose.

A woman! In the prison yard! The sound was taken up by the inmates of the Dungeon Block. Even though they could not see what was going on, the word had spread and their response was blood-chilling, primitive.

Nancy Chisholm was aware of all this, for color had left her face. But she went ahead with her purpose.

"You can't do this, Mr. Ledge!" she said. "This is torture. You know that the warden told you after the last case that you must never—!"

"This is no concern of yours, miss," Ledge said.

She stood her ground. "If this man is to be punished, the warden will decide the penalty," she said. "This is not your responsibility. Take him back to his cell and handle the matter through the usual channels."

She stared Ledge down. He was crimson with fury. He tried to stall, but finally nodded to Coulter. "All right. We don't want the lady to be put out with us, now do we, Pete. Take the scum away."

He forced a grin. "I was only tryin' to throw a little fright into him, miss. He's too bold. A bad one."

She turned and headed back toward the door from which she had come. Wild, jackal-like howling arose and swelled. She began to hurry. To run. She vanished through the door as though pursued by the devil.

Matt was returned to his cell. Ledge hit him across the thighs with a club as he was pushed into the cage.

The next day he was marched to the warden's office. Tom Chisholm was strictly official, treating him as though he was only the number by which he was addressed.

"You're charged with insubordination in the mess hall," he said. "Ten days in the dungeon on bread and water. This is your second major offense. I warn you that you've reached your limit. You'll regret it if you're brought here a third time."

Matt, seething, went back to the dungeon. This time he had as companions a Cocopah Indian who had tried to kill another convict in a moment of frenzy and a sullen criminal who had been caught trying to smuggle the metal handle from a laundry vat. The handle would have been converted into a weapon.

This convict was known as Big Jim. "There's a big bustout comin'," he told Matt.

That was all he would say at the time. But long afterward— it might have been a week later, for Matt had quit trying to keep track of time—Big Jim spoke again. "It's Tom Chisholm that sent me to Stone Lodge when he was sheriff in Cedar County. I'll put a knife or a bullet in his guts before I go over the wall if it's the last thing I ever do."

Time passed, and there was no bustout. Matt's term in the dungeon ended. He returned to the ranks of the faceless men, marched with them, ate with them, listened to their mutterings. Without really seeing them, without really hearing them. Nor did they seem to see him or listen to his own murmurings.

However there was one difference. He was no longer persecuted by Ledge for petty infractions. He was sure it was not because of any softening of the man's dislike of him. But Ledge apparently had decided to ignore him. Matt could think of only one explanation. Nancy Chisholm. She must have interceded for him with her father.

One morning Doc Diamond spoke in his ear as they marched to breakfast. "It won't be long now. Are you with us?"

"Only if you know what you're doing," Matt murmured.

"I know," Diamond said. "And it's sure. I've got a ticket that will let us out—right through the gate."

That was all Diamond would say. Matt discovered that Ledge had been looking directly at them. The guard captain must certainly have known they had been whispering in line, a breach of discipline that usually meant at least a week in the kitchen or the laundry. But Ledge's brassy features remained blank. Even his eyes turned away.

From that moment, Matt sensed a change in this place of lost men. Like the first stirring of life. The undercurrent at Stone Lodge was no longer slow. It was now feverish.

He desperately wanted to get word to Tom Chisholm. He even thought of using Ledge as a messenger, but an inner voice cautioned him against trusting even the guard captain.

He was forced to bide his time until Chisholm appeared in the mess hall on an inspection trip.

He looked at Chisholm only once, and permitted no expression to cross his face. But the very stoniness of his stare was enough. Chisholm moved away, but Matt caught the flicker of acknowledgment in his eyes.

Chisholm held an unannounced inspection of Dungeon Block that same night. He paused at each cell, speaking to each inmate, hearing grievances and occasionally entering a cell for closer view of the interior. Two guards accompanied him, remaining outside with cocked buckshot guns.

Chisholm finally arrived at Matt's cell and peered between the bars. "Any complaints, 1571?" he asked.

Matt, who was lying on the bunk, did not answer. Chisholm ordered the guards to open the cell door. Matt got sullenly to his feet, backed to the wall and stood at attention as required.

Chisholm entered and turned back the mattress, pretending to search the cell. He came close to Matt. Matt spoke in a mere murmur. "It's coming soon. Can't tell exactly when."

Chisholm said loudly, "At least you keep the place cleaner than most. I'll note it on your record. You can stand a good mark or two."

In a murmur: "How do they aim to go over the wall?"

"Diamond said something about going out the gate. He said he had a sure ticket."

"All right," Chisholm said for the benefit of the two guards outside. "Maybe we can make a decent person of you in time, Battles."

"Watch out for Big Jim," Matt breathed. "He's gone off his rocker. Been cooped up too long. All he can think of is killing you for having him sent up."

Chisholm nodded and left the cell, continuing his inspection. Presently he left Dungeon Block. Once again the ominous quiet descended.

Each morning the squad of trusties straggled out through the gate, bearing tools to harvest the crops in the cultivated fields below the bluff along the river. The clodhoppers, the other convicts called them. They were accompanied only by two guards who had shotguns listlessly slung on their arms. It was rare indeed when a clodhopper attempted to go over the hill.

Each morning the kitchen and laundry squads marched sullenly into the infernos. This duty was reserved for the Dungeon Squad exclusively while the remainder of the inmates labored in the broom shop amid dust and straw.

Matt was serving a week's time in the kitchen crew. One of his companions in the glare of the bake ovens to which they had been assigned was the lowering, heavy-jawed Turk Shagrue.

Kitchen duty at least gave more opportunity for exchange of words, for the guards kept their distance from the heat of the ovens. The clatter

147

of activity covered their muted conversation.

For a day or two, Shagrue worked alongside Matt without saying anything of any significance.

"Kin you swim?" Shagrue finally muttered one morning as they handled long spatulas at the ovens where bread was baking.

Matt did not answer for minutes, during which he lifted flats of hot, fresh-baked loaves from the ovens and swung them onto wooden racks to cool.

"Better than a stone," he said. "Not as fast as a fish."

"How about rowin' a boat?"

"Tried it once or twice. I'm the kind that likes a horse to do my traveling."

"A horse leaves tracks," Shagrue said.

It was another day before Shagrue spoke again. "Doc says fer the four o' us to stick close together when we spring it."

"When will that be?"

"Nobody knows but Doc. He don't take chances on somebody turnin' snitch."

"What about the rest of 'em?" Matt asked.

"The rest of who?"

"The cons."

Shagrue gave him a scornful glare. "To hell with 'em. All Doc wants is for them to keep the guards busy while we cut out."

That was all the information he could gain from the man. Shagrue would not open his lips again on the matter of the bustout.

Matt's term in the kitchen ended and he went back to helping with the cleanup squad. He had learned a few things at least. The prison break was still on and a boat or boats were a part of Diamond's escape plan. That meant the river, of course. The Buffalo's channel curved past the prison, passing within a hundred yards or so of the base of the bluff on which the stone walls stood. It was born in the mountains, but was wider and tamer here, as it flattened out on the plains. It flowed southward past Stone Lodge but veered northward in a wide loop and eventually emptied into the Missouri River some seventy or eighty miles north.

The next afternoon, as he moved through the yard during the exercise period when the convicts were allowed to drop rigid discipline for twenty minutes, Diamond passed by him, brushing shoulders.

"Look under your bunk, Battles. Be ready any time. Maybe tonight. Maybe tomorrow. We need rain, clouds."

Matt looked up at the open sky. Clouds were moving in. The sun was darkening. By afternoon it was raining. A persistent, driving rain that brought grateful coolness and revived a parched land.

After lights out, Matt searched beneath the bunk in his cell. He finally found it. A loaded six-shooter! His fingertips told him in the darkness that the handle was battered and nicked from much use, but it undoubtedly could fire bullets that would kill. It was loaded, and with it were a handful of extra shells.

The gun had been concealed along the inner frame of the bunk, out of sight, but in a place where its discovery would have been almost certain during one of the frequent searches that were a routine part of the guards' duty.

That meant it had been placed there only recently, probably during the supper hour when the cells were empty. By whom? All cells were locked when the inmates were absent.

It was hardly possible that Diamond could have performed that feat of magic. There was only one answer. He had inside help. One, or perhaps more, of Tom Chisholm's guards had been bought off.

Bought off with what? There was but one answer to that too. Money. And probably money that was realized from sale of the train robbery bullion. If so, it meant that a fourth person had been in on the train holdup. And that might be the person who was furnishing the funds for what was happening here at Stone Lodge.

Johnny Kidd! Johnny the Kid! Was he the one? Matt tried to put that ugly thought out of his mind. There must be some other explanation.

It occurred to him that there must be other guns in the hands of convicts. There was no telling how many. Men like Big Jim, perhaps. Men who bore blind grudges and who would not hesitate to kill to pay off for wrongs, fancied or real.

Matt seized his tincup and began pounding on the iron bars. A guard shouted a harsh order to quiet down. When Matt failed to obey, the guard came striding to the cell, carrying a long goad which was used to keep beserk prisoners at bay.

"What's eatin' you?" the man snarled. "Stop that cussed racket!"

"I want to see the warden," Matt said.

"Oh, so it's the warden you want to see, an' at this time of night," the guard raged. "You'll see him, but not before tomorrow, an' you'll likely go back to the snake pit for this little—"

"It's important!" Matt whispered.

He knew that it might spoil everything, give away the fact that he was planted to gain Diamond's confidence, but he had to try to warn Chisholm that there had been treachery and that many of the convicts were armed.

"What's so important about it?" the guard demanded. "Now be quiet or—"

Somewhere in the depths of the prison a six-shooter exploded. Doc Diamond's voice sounded. "Here we go, boys! Everybody!"

The prison was silent for the time it takes for a man to draw a long, deep breath. Then bedlam broke loose. Guns opened up. Convicts were screeching and rattling cell bars.

151

The guard turned and ran away in stumbling haste. Flashes of powderflame danced in the rainswept prison yard. The reports echoed in Dungeon Block.

The shooting tapered off. But it was only a momentary lull. Matt heard the heavy sound of men in motion. The prison yard seemed to be filled with convicts who had been released from their cells in the other blocks.

Running feet pounded in Dungeon Block. Cell doors were being hurled open. Doc Diamond appeared at Matt's cell.

"Come on!" he panted. "Hurry!"

He swung open the door of the cell. It had not been locked! Matt realized that must have been the case all through the prison.

He thrust the smuggled six-shooter into the band of his striped breeches and raced with Diamond out of the block and into the open yard.

Convicts were milling around. Rain beat down from sullen clouds that hung over the mountain ridges. Many of the felons seemed bewildered, not knowing what to do next. They were awaiting leadership. Others were wild with glee. They were howling and brandishing weapons. Some had pistols. The majority were armed with knives and clubs.

One wild-eyed convict with a six-shooter was Big Jim the sullen one. "This way, you dungeon lice!" he was screaming. "Let's git the big augur.

Git Chisholm! We'll dig him out'n his fine, fancy office where he sets an' sends people like us to the snake pit!"

Other men joined Big Jim as he headed toward the iron door that led to the warden's quarters.

"Look out fer the Gatlin'!" someone screeched.

Matt's gaze shifted to the high tower. The maw of the Gatling was swinging into position to pour slugs into the prison yard.

Matt started to head for cover, but Diamond's hand grasped his arm, halting him. "Don't worry about the Gatling!" Diamond shouted. "It's jammed."

Matt could see the gunner in the tower working frantically at the breech of the weapon. Big Jim lifted his pistol and fired. The gunner was hit and dropped from sight.

Another guard, who was opening fire with a rifle from a parapet, dropped his rifle, clasped at his stomach and fell. It was Turk Shagrue who had fired that shot. He and Frank Welton had appeared and joined Matt and Diamond.

"Stick together!" Diamond said. "Not too fast. Wait! Let the others clear the way. We're going out that way too. It's the easiest path. Right through the warden's house."

CHAPTER NINE

The majority of the guards had taken to cover, realizing, no doubt, that it was useless to attempt to stem the tide in the prison yard. At least two guards, unable to escape, had been seized. Matt saw them go down under a rain of blows from weapons and fists.

Big Jim and his followers were pounding at the door that led to the warden's office. The door swung open so suddenly that Big Jim plunged forward, landing on his face in the hall.

The door had been left unbarred. Like the weapons that had been planted in the cells, like the keys with which Diamond and Shagrue and Welton had released the horde of convicts, it was part of the treachery.

Matt started to head in that direction, but again Diamond held him back. "Wait, I say!" Diamond rasped. "Let those fools lead the way."

Matt tried to pull away. He still wanted to warn Tom Chisholm. But he was already too late to save the warden's life. Chisholm had appeared in the hallway beyond the open door. He had six-shooters in his hands. He was in his shirt sleeves and evidently had come racing from his living quarters.

He was lifting the guns and shouting what must

have been an order for the convicts to throw down their weapons. Matt could not hear the words in the uproar.

"Look out!" he groaned. "Big Jim will kill you!" He could not even hear his own voice.

Big Jim came to his knees from his sprawling fall. Laughing savagely he lifted his pistol and opened fire, emptying the gun almost at pointblank range into the warden's body.

Tom Chisholm was hurled back by the impact of the slugs. He slumped against the rear wall, blood spurting from his wounds. He grimly clung to life long enough to fire one shot. That bullet struck Big Jim in the forehead and Matt saw the horrifying damage it did as it emerged.

Big Jim was killed almost instantly, but Tom Chisholm was dead also as he slid to the floor, the smoking six-shooter still in his right hand.

Nancy Chisholm came into the hall. She threw herself on her father's body to protect him from further bullets. She was screaming in horror.

"Come on!" Diamond shouted. "There's the ticket I mentioned. Our ticket out of this place."

He raced ahead of Matt into the hallway, leaping over Big Jim's body. Nancy sprang to her feet as though realizing his intention and fled through the door from which she had entered the hall.

Diamond was at her heels, preventing her from closing and locking the door. He pursued her into the rooms she and her father had been using as living quarters. Matt was only a stride behind him.

She was brought to bay when she was blocked by a door she could not open in time. Diamond seized her around the waist and swung her off her feet.

Matt jammed a shoulder against Diamond, shoving him against the wall with the girl still in his arms. "Let her go!" he said. "I don't stand for roughing women. Put her down."

Turk Shagrue and Frank Welton had followed them and had closed doors in the faces of the other convicts so that there was only the four of them. And the girl.

"Take a look out there!" Diamond panted. He pointed with the muzzle of his .45 toward a window.

The room in which he had overtaken the girl apparently was a living room. It was furnished with chairs and a davenport and had rugs on the maple floor. The windows and the main door of the house opened on the landscaped area at the front of the main gate of the prison. The lamps still burned on the prison walls lighting this foreground.

Matt could see the shadowy figures of prison guards in the open area, moving among the trees and using the shrubs as cover. They were flanking the warden's house. It was evident they knew their principal quarry was in the house.

"We'll have to make it out of the place in some other direction," Matt said. "They'll riddle us if we show up out there."

"No," Diamond said. "This is the way I told you we'd go. The easiest way."

"There must be a dozen men out there—" Matt began.

"Here's our free ticket," Diamond said.

He still grasped Nancy Chisholm. She was ashen with terror, but was determinedly struggling to free herself although she was no match for Diamond's strength.

"My father!" she gasped. "He's been shot! He needs help! Please—!"

"There's nothing you can do for him," Diamond said. "He's dead and good riddance. But there's plenty you can do for us."

Her eyes swung to Matt, seeking the truth. He said nothing, but she saw the answer in his face. For the first time she weakened, stricken by horror and grief.

"You—you killed him?" she asked Diamond, her voice high-pitched.

"No," Diamond said impatiently. "Big Jim got him. What difference who did it? Come along now. We're going out there. You're going with us."

"Me? Oh, no."

"If they start shooting you'll be the first to stop

a slug," Diamond said. "Do you understand what I'm saying?"

She suddenly began fighting to escape with new fury and strength, and managed to partly wrest herself from Diamond's grasp. But Shagrue and Welton moved in and restrained her.

Diamond's thin face was bloodless, his eyes cold, deadly. "Listen to me," he said to her. "And you can believe that I'll do exactly as I say I will. Go along with us, cause no trouble, and you'll stay alive. That's your only chance. If you don't, I'll kill you and carry you with us anyway. They won't know the difference. They won't shoot. We're going out there with you as insurance against them opening up on us. Dead or alive, you're going. Take your choice, and do it now."

Diamond had jammed his cocked .45 into her side. Matt had remained silent, waiting a chance to interfere, to snatch her out of Diamond's grasp, kill the man if necessary. But it was impossible. Any such move would almost surely mean that Diamond would pull the trigger and she would die.

He tried another tack. "I'll hold onto her," he said to Diamond. "You do the talking to the guards." All he could hope for was to protect her from any shooting that might start.

Even that failed. "I'll do the talking—*and* the holding," Diamond snapped. "Come on! Here we go!"

Nancy Chisholm had given up her resistance, knowing it was useless. Diamond, an arm clamped around her waist, held her in front of him as a shield as he walked to the door and opened it. He stood there, a six-shooter in his right hand, holding the girl.

Silence clapped down over the open area, although the shouting and some shooting continued inside the prison where convicts were swarming over the rear walls and fleeing into the darkness.

"We're coming out!" Diamond shouted. "We've got the warden's daughter. She won't be hurt unless you want it that way. Any bullets you send in our direction will have to go through her first."

He paused, letting that sink in. The silence of the guards seemed to deepen.

The irony of it came home to Matt. With Tom Chisholm dead and his daughter standing a good chance of being killed also within the next few minutes, there would be no person left alive who knew the real story of the events that had sent him to Stone Lodge.

His helplessness appalled him. For there was no way of interfering without bringing on her death. At the moment, at least. For Diamond would kill her without hesitation if he chose.

"Stick tight around me," Diamond said. "They won't shoot. Here we go!"

He again yelled to the guards that they were coming out and that the girl would die if shooting started. He led the way from the door, holding Nancy as a shield. Matt tried to place himself between her and any possible bullet that might come in case some guard had a nervous trigger finger.

"Get back of us, Battles!" Diamond rasped. "Get out of the way, I say!"

Matt knew Diamond would shoot him if he balked. Gunplay would likely mean the death of them all, for the chances were it would touch off the suppressed storm around them. He dropped back a pace.

For a space, the only sound was the thud of their shoes and their heavy breathing as they ran. They passed within arm's reach of one of the guards, who was sheltered back of shrubbery, a rifle in his hands.

The man did not fire. He remained motionless and let them race past.

"Don't follow us!" Diamond shouted over his shoulder. "Stay back."

He was carrying Nancy bodily. They descended from the prison hill into the dark streets of the town. Diamond seemed to be following some route that had been mapped for him and which he had memorized, for he kept peering around, marking out bearing points as he followed a twisting course.

The uproar at the prison had awakened the town and Matt saw faces appear at doors and windows as they raced past. But no opposition came.

Diamond, gasping, set Nancy on her feet. "Give me a hand with her, Battles!" he panted. "I'm bushed."

Matt found himself custodian of the girl. He grasped her arm, hurrying her along as they continued their flight. With Shagrue and Welton right at their heels he did not dare attempt to give her a chance to attempt escape. They would only seize her. And that would bring on the shooting between them and himself that he was trying to avoid.

They were all feeling the pace and had slowed to a fast walk. Nancy was reeling, gasping in exhaustion. Matt put an arm around her, half-carrying her.

The sheds and corrals of a wagon freighting outfit loomed on the fringe of town. Horses and mules were moving about and snorting in the corrals, excited by the noise in the distance and by the scent of approaching humans.

Acting on what evidently was a part of the prearranged plan, Diamond, Welton, and Shagrue tumbled down the bars of the corral gates and stampeded the animals into the open. Fanning their hats, they sent them scattering into the brush and darkness away from town. There must have been forty animals or more in the stampede and they vanished into the rainy night, hoofs spattering mud and water.

"That'll give 'em something to think about," Diamond panted. "This way! They won't know but what we had saddle horses under us."

He led the way in a scramble down the low cutbank into the flood channel of the river. They stumbled through dry sand bars and weeds that were flourishing on hummocks in the shallow backwater.

Presently Matt realized they were following a beaten path. The main channel of the river appeared ahead. Willows and cottonwoods found foothold on higher hummocks. Matt understood that the path they had followed was used in trailing stock to the river to be watered.

Diamond pulled up, his lungs laboring. "It must be close around here," he wheezed.

Shagrue and Welton waded into the margin of the river and were delving among willows on either side of the trail. "Here it is!" Shagrue panted triumphantly. "Jest like he said."

He and Welton returned, pushing a boat. Matt saw that it was a sizeable river skiff, with seats for two oarsmen. Oars were already in place in the locks. Someone had hidden the craft there for their use.

"All right!" Diamond said hoarsely. "Everybody aboard! Hustle!"

They could not have run much farther. He had

continued to half-carry Nancy Chisholm. His lungs were on fire. Diamond caught the girl by the arms and dragged her knee-deep into the river, pushing her toward the floating skiff.

"Climb into the boat, my lady," he said. "You're still going with us. Climb in, I say!"

Sobbing, she tried to fight free of his grasp. Diamond holstered the six-shooter he had in his hand and lifted his arm to deliver a blow into her face.

Matt caught the upraised arm, sending Diamond reeling back off balance. Only the nearby skiff saved him from sprawling in the water.

"I tell you there's to be no roughing of women," Matt said.

Diamond was silent for an instant. Then he decided that this was no time to make an issue of it. They could hear sounds in the distance. The stampede of the freighters' stock had confused the bulk of the pursuers, but there were also indications that horsemen were approaching the river.

"Get her in the boat, then," Diamond snarled.

Matt lifted the girl into the skiff. Diamond and the others were already shoving the craft toward deeper water. The four men pulled themselves aboard, their weight causing the craft to heel dangerously. They righted the skiff and averted swamping.

The current swung the craft around. The rain

had ended suddenly and the clouds were lifting. They were still so near the prison that the lights on the walls were bright in the distance and the clouds still reflected their glow dimly over the river.

Frank Welton was alone in the prow, a target apart from the others who were crowded in the waist of the craft.

A rifle opened up on the brushy shore from which they had fled. Three shots were fired by some marksman who had seen a chance to shoot without endangering the girl. Matt heard the soggy sound as one of the bullets tore through flesh.

Welton uttered a strangled gasp and collapsed into the bottom of the boat. "I'm hit, Doc!" he mumbled.

Shagrue was swinging one pair of oars, driving the blades deep into the river in an attempt to carry them out of range of the rifleman,

"Grab the other oars, Battles!" Diamond said. "Row!"

Matt took over the second set of sweeps. The skiff surged forward. The lights faded into the distance. No more shots came.

Welton lay huddled in the narrow prow. He tried to say something, but could only utter choking sounds.

Nancy worked her way past Matt and Shagrue and reached Welton's side. "He's badly wounded," she said. "You must go back to shore."

Diamond swore savagely. "And be strung up!" he said. "Keep rowing. Frank, I'll take a look at you in a minute. Right now, we've got to get the hell out of here."

Diamond knelt, facing Shagrue and added his strength to the oars. Matt also bent to the task. There was shouting on shore. The pursuers evidently knew that at least one convict had been hit. But it was also evident they had lost sight of the skiff in the darkness.

The boat had reached mid-river and a strong current helped put distance between them and Stone Lodge. The shouting faded. Soon, all they could hear was the slap of their oars in the river.

"All right," Diamond said. "We're out of the worst of it. Take a rest and drift for a while."

Matt and Shagrue sagged, utterly spent. Diamond edged past them into the prow. He pushed Nancy aside and bent over Frank Welton.

"You should have known better than to make a target of yourself, Frank," he said after a moment. "You were foolish."

Welton tried to make himself understood in his bubbling voice. "My God, Doc! You don't mean I'm going to croak!"

"I can't tell for sure here in the dark," Diamond said, "but I'm afraid you got it through the lung, Frank."

Welton's voice shrilled. "Do something, Doc! You know how. You're a doctor. I ain't going to die. You got to help me."

"I'm sorry, Frank," Diamond said. "There's nothing I can do. Nothing any doctor can do."

Welton was silent for a space, and so were all the listeners. "You don't mean that, Doc," Welton sobbed. But he knew that Diamond did mean it.

"Put me ashore, Doc," Welton said, his voice pleading. "Give me a chance. They'll find me. Take me to a doctor. The prison doctor. Maybe he can fix me up."

"Sure, Frank," Diamond said. "We'll put you ashore. Right now."

Instead, Diamond lifted the dying man and tossed him overside into the river. Before Matt realized what was coming, Diamond drew his six-shooter, leaned over the prow, placed the muzzle against Welton's body as it came to the surface, and pulled the trigger.

The explosion was muffled to a heavy thud by the soaked shirt of the victim. A blast of spray and powdersmoke swirled around the boat.

Welton tenaciously fought off death for a moment, spurred by the raging desire to take Diamond with him. He clawed at the side of the skiff. "Damn you, Doc!" he sobbed. "I'll—"

Diamond jabbed the muzzle of the six-shooter against him and pushed him away from the boat.

There seemed to be genuine regret in Diamond's voice. "Don't you remember, Frank? We all agreed we'd leave nobody alive if he got hit. You agreed to it. Turk agreed to it. I agreed to it. You might have lived long enough to talk if they found you on shore. They might have made you talk. So long, pal. I'm sorry."

Welton remained floating on the dark surface. But he was face-down. Then, slowly, his body sank from sight.

Shagrue swung the oars again, propelling the skiff hurriedly away from that place. Diamond dried the muzzle of his six-shooter and placed a fresh shell in place of the one he had emptied.

"I'll spell you at the oars, Battles," he said, his voice as cool as though he was discussing the weather. "You better look after the lady."

Nancy Chisholm had fainted. She lay huddled in the bottom of the boat. Matt dipped water from the river, moistening her throat and forehead. She moved and sighed. Then she began to weep. Grief for her father. Horror for Frank Welton whose grave was in the dark river.

She tried to sit up and failed. Matt lifted her to the narrow seat in the prow and supported her until she strengthened.

From far, far away on the east shore a man shouted, the words telegraphed by the river's surface. "Put Miss Chisholm ashore, Diamond. We know you've got her. We'll follow you to

168

eternity. You can't get away. If any harm comes to her, it'll only go worse for you."

"Quiet!" Diamond murmured. "Stop rowing. They're only trying to find out where we are. They can't see us."

They drifted for a long time. The men on the far shore finally went silent.

After a time Diamond spoke. "All right. We'll head upstream."

"*Up*stream?" Shagrue asked, startled.

"They'll be expecting us to go in the other direction with the current. There are swamps and backwater along the shore above Stone Lodge where we'll hole up. We can make it downriver some other night when they won't be expecting it."

Nancy had straightened and was listening. She pushed away Matt's hand which was supporting her. "I can take care of myself," she said. "Keep your hands off me."

"I'll be glad to," Matt said. "I'm not exactly in the habit of trying to honey up to a fainting female, if that's what you're thinking."

"Shut up, both of you!" Diamond hissed furiously. "Don't you realize that voices carry a long way on water?"

She drew a deep breath. Matt realized that she intended to scream a warning that the fugitives were turning upriver in the hope men were still listening on the far shore.

He seized her, clapping a hand over her mouth. Her attempt ended in a gasping gurgle. She had courage. Too much, perhaps. She must have known she probably was throwing away her life in attempting to make that outcry. She had just seen Diamond murder in cold blood a man who had been his comrade. He had slain Frank Welton to make sure the man would not live long enough to tell where the loot from the train robbery had been hidden. She must surely know that her own life was worth even less to Diamond.

She continued to struggle in Matt's grasp. He held her helpless. "Will you be good now!" he rasped. In her ear, he whispered, "You little fool! Do you want to get us both killed?"

She subsided abruptly. Matt loosened his grip, and permitted her to talk. "All right," she said.

"Gag her!" Diamond ordered.

"That's not needed," Matt said. "She just said she'd keep quiet."

"And I say to gag her!" Diamond said. There was again the deadly savagery in his voice. "Or tie it tight enough around her damned throat to shut her up for keeps. I don't care which."

"Gag her with what?" Matt asked.

"How do I know?" Diamond raged. "Tear her waist off and use that."

Matt compromised by ripping the sleeve from the blouse she was wearing.

"Open up," he said. "You brought this on

170

yourself. You'll be no use to us dead. Or to anybody. But that's where you'll be if you try to buck off the saddle again."

She surely must know what he really meant. She must be aware that she was his only corroborating witness if he ever got out of this alive.

She evidently knew what was in his mind. That seemed to anger her. She defiantly kept her teeth clamped shut, refusing to submit to being gagged. Then she seemed to think better of it and permitted him to place the rolled length of cloth between her teeth.

Matt allowed plenty of slack so that she would not be unduly uncomfortable. But a gag, under any circumstances, could be only slow torture when endured for hours, and that was what she faced. Even that attempt to help her failed, for Diamond inspected the gag, jerked it brutally tight and said to Matt, "Quit being soft."

There were two filled gunnysacks in the boat. One contained a supply of food, along with battered cooking utensils. Also two rifles and three six-shooters to add to their armament, and boxes of shells.

The other bag held clothing with which to replace their convict stripes—cheap cotton shirts, jeans, and even felt hats. The person who had provided the means of escape and the skiff had made a thorough job of preparation.

Diamond tossed a hat and garments to Matt. "These ought to be about your size," he said. "Let's all get rid of the stripes right now. Even at night they can be spotted quite a distance."

Matt knew that he had inherited the garb intended for Frank Welton. Dead man's clothing.

Diamond bound Nancy's hands at her back, using strips he ripped from the discarded prison uniforms.

"That's so she can't loosen that gag and let out a squawl," he said.

"What if this boat upsets?" Matt inquired. "She wouldn't have a chance."

"That," Diamond said, "would be mighty bad luck for her."

CHAPTER TEN

Rowing cautiously so as to make as little sound as possible, they pushed upstream, hugging the brushy west shore. The faint lights of Stone Lodge drew abreast, glinting on the surface of the river.

Sounds still drifted. Yells and screams. An occasional shot. The Gatling gun opened up, firing a dozen rounds, the sound heavy and ominous. Evidently the weapon had been repaired or a substitute found.

"Good!" Diamond said. "Sounds like some of the cons have holed up in a block and are fighting it out. That'll keep a lot of the guards too busy to worry about us for a while."

"But not all of 'em," Shagrue said dubiously. "Not when we've stole a female."

"If we hadn't taken her we'd be lying dead back there in front of that calaboose," Diamond snapped. "You know that. I'm sick of you and Battles belly-aching about how I handled this. We're out, aren't we? And we're going to stay out."

They pushed ahead. They had been moving upstream at least an hour, Matt calculated, and there had been no sign of danger. The hour must be nearing midnight, and Diamond was urging more speed.

"We've got to be off the river and hid in the

173

brush above town before daybreak," he kept saying.

The storm was moving eastward. Stars were beginning to show to the west. A dank, humid heat came in, ending the space of coolness. And another hazard appeared in the shape of a railroad bridge that spanned the river.

"They've likely got somebody on that bridge to make sure we don't do just what we're trying to do," Matt said.

This was a probability that Diamond had apparently overlooked. He seemed to be at a loss. They drifted while he considered their next move.

A train whistle sounded to the east. Matt remembered that his arrival at Stone Lodge, handcuffed to Tom Chisholm, had been at about this same time of night.

"That's probably a westbound passenger, and it won't make more than a quick stop at the station, if it stops at all," he said. "If they've sent anybody to the bridge to keep watch, I'm willing to bet he's crossed to this west side. He can't stay on the bridge with a train coming, and they're not likely to expect us to pass by along that east shore, for that's practically right under the walls of the prison."

He added, "I say to shift to the other side, and row like hell while the train is crossing the bridge. It'll make enough noise to cover any sounds we make."

"We'll try it," Diamond said.

The plan worked. Rowing strongly, they swung the skiff to the east shore, moved cautiously to within a pistol shot of the bridge. The prison loomed on the bluff almost above them, so near they could hear the ricochet of the occasional rifleshots that were being fired by the guards and the defiant yells of the barricaded convicts.

They heard the train steam into the station in town. It remained there for a few minutes. Its whistle wailed and it groaned into motion, heading for the bridge.

They bent to the oars, rowing furiously, and passed under the bridge as the train rumbled overhead. They were upstream and rounding the bend beyond the bluff on which the prison stood before the roar of the train had faded into the night west of the river. If there really had been anyone on watch at the bridge he apparently had failed to sight them.

They continued upstream, easing off the oars. Their mood changed. Shagrue began chattering with almost hysterical joy, rebounding from the tension that had held them for hours. Diamond cautioned him to quiet down, but the savagery had faded even from his manner.

"It's safe now to take the bit out of the filly's teeth," Matt said.

Without waiting for Diamond's approval, he removed the gag from Nancy. She mumbled numbly, "If you'll cut my hands loose I'll promise not to scratch or claw."

Matt freed her wrists. She sat massaging her throat and wrists, restoring circulation. "Thanks," she said dryly. "I'll have more sympathy for a horse from now on."

She was still displaying more courage than prudence. She was refusing to show fear. She must surely realize that she was valuable to Diamond only up to a point. Once Diamond was sure she was no longer needed as a shield he might decide she was only a burden and a danger. Also that she knew too much.

Matt nudged her, giving her a glare, trying to subdue her. She ignored him, and he raged inwardly.

Even so, he couldn't help thinking of Jeff Rossiter and envying him. Nancy Chisholm would make life mighty lively for any man she married. If she lived.

If she lived! He forced himself to quit thinking.

He took his turn at the oars. Keeping close to shore, they were mainly in backwater, with little current to buck. The dank, musty smell of swamps and mud flats increased as they progressed up the river. The lights of Stone Lodge had long since faded back of them. The last of the clouds had vanished and the stars glittered overhead once more.

Those stars were growing pale as the first

promise of daybreak tinged the east when Diamond said, "There's some sort of an opening in the brush ahead. Swing in. We can't risk hunting for a better place with daylight coming."

Thick brush matted a swampy shore. The skiff entered a slough of scum-covered, brackish water. Mosquitoes settled on them in swarms. Water lapped dismally at the prow. The oars became clogged with slimy moss. A bullfrog broke into hoarse voice, startling all three men into reaching for their guns. They subsided grimly, their nerves still taut.

Dawn strengthened and allowed them to make out their surroundings. They were in the midst of a gloomy swamp. Rotting driftwood festooned the hummocks. Water snakes etched fast-moving ripples on the scummy surface as they sped to cover.

Diamond, after some false halts, picked out a hiding place on a willow-grown hummock that stood slightly higher than the surroundings and offered a small stretch of reasonably dry sand. They waded ashore and pulled the skiff into hiding among reeds.

A stiff breeze had sprung up, rattling the brush. It was a hot wind, but it conferred at least one blessing. It drove the swarms of mosquitoes and gnats to cover.

The food supply consisted of salt meat, flour, coffee, and tins of meat and vegetables. Diamond opened corned beef and tomatoes which they ate cold, for he would not permit the lighting of a fire.

He offered food to Nancy, but she refused.

Matt spoke. "Eat! You'll need something in your belly before this is over."

She gave him a surprised look. He had meant to shock her. Even as a child she had detested vulgarity. She had fallen into an apathetic acceptance of her situation in the last few hours. Reaction, weariness and, above all, grief for her father had numbed her.

Matt wanted to stir her out of her morbid memories. She wearily took from his hand the food that she would not touch when Diamond had offered it. He saw the thin, bitter smile of resentment on Diamond's lips.

She ate with the daintiness of her upbringing and Diamond watched her slim fingers with fascination. Also Shagrue. She became aware of this. She shivered a little. Matt found that her gaze had swung to him. She seemed to find assurance there.

She sat primly, trying to maintain dignity and calmness even in her damp, wrinkled garments which clung to her, even with her hair hanging loose down her back. There was an inner wholesomeness in her, a spotlessness of character and mind. But she was a woman— young and desirable and that was what Diamond and Shagrue were seeing in her.

Matt spoke gruffly to her. "You sleep in the boat. The rest of us will sleep on the ground."

Diamond started to speak, angered by the way Matt was usurping authority. Then he shrugged, again deciding that the time and place to make an issue of it had not yet arrived.

He bowed with mocking deference to Nancy and made a sweeping gesture toward the boat. "Your boudoir, my lady. I trust you will rest well. I'll have the butler call you when we are ready to leave."

He added, still smiling thinly, "I also trust that you don't walk in your sleep, or that you do not decide to leave us without thanking us for our hospitality. I would be offended. Deeply."

She moved silently into the boat, frightened, and huddled down in the craft. Matt arranged a covering of willow branches above her so as to shade her from the rising sun.

He picked a sleeping place for himself beneath the willows in a position where neither Diamond nor Shagrue could approach the skiff without stepping over him.

Diamond took note of this. He smiled scornfully. "Don't let the sight of a petticoat turn your head, Battles," he said.

"We all will keep our hands off her," Matt said.

Diamond nodded. "Exactly. We've got too much at stake to begin squabbling over a girl. The world's full of girls."

"See to it that you be the first to remember that, Battles," Shagrue said.

"Meaning what?" Matt demanded.

Diamond answered that. "Meaning that you are showing signs of being smitten by the charms of a lady in distress."

Matt glanced toward the boat. No doubt their words were reaching the ears of Nancy Chisholm, but there was no sign of it beneath the brushy covering.

"She's not the kind that appeals to me," he said. "It's just that she's as good as a sheet of boiler plate between us and any posse that might happen to cut our trail. We've already proved that. Let's continue to look on it that way."

"You ain't the only one that's smitten," Shagrue grinned. "As I heard it in the Lodge, she's already spoken for by a man what's knee-deep in money. Name of Jeff Rossiter. Everybody on the Hill seen him comin' around right regular, wearin' his courtin' smile."

Diamond, who had settled down on a sleeping place, lifted his head. "Rossiter?" he echoed. "Of the cattle family?"

"That's right," Shagrue said.

Diamond lay thinking for a time. "Maybe we've hit another little streak of pay dirt that might pan out," he finally said musingly.

"How's that?" Shagrue asked.

"Maybe Rossiter might be happy to get his

sweetheart back safe and sound for—say ten thousand dollars. Or, let's say, twenty thousand. That'd be piker money for his family, from what I've been told."

"You don't mean that," Matt said.

"Money's money," Diamond replied. "Wherever you find it."

"Kidnaping for ransom is the best way I know of to get into real trouble," Matt said.

"You can only look up a rope once," Diamond said. "Don't forget that they'll hold us responsible for the warden's death."

"It isn't quite that simple," Matt said. "They can only hang you for that, and for using a woman as a shield. But for asking ransom, they've got other ideas. Indian ideas."

Shagrue twisted around, glaring. "Torture?"

"With improvements by white men," Matt said.

"They've got to catch us first," Diamond said. "And they never will. I admit that we're through in this country. What we've got to do is scrape together all the cash we can get our hands on and run for Canada."

"That won't be far enough," Matt said.

"You're right. But it'll be easier to get somewhere else by way of Canada. Me, I intend to wind up in South America. Maybe Brazil. Where it's warm all the year around. Where the Portuguese gals are said to be mighty pretty. And no extradition treaties with the United States. But if I go south I want enough money to live easy the rest of my life. Like a gentlemen should live."

"Ten thousand split among the three of us wouldn't make gentlemen of us," Matt said. "Nor even twenty thousand."

Shagrue entered the conversation. "Four of us."

Matt's brows lifted. "Four? How come?"

Diamond again lifted his head and gave Shagrue a glare. "Who do you suppose gave us all that help in breaking out of Stone Lodge?" he said impatiently. "Santa Claus?"

"I can guess," Matt said. "And it wasn't Santa Claus. So that cuts the pie that much thinner."

"You can fatten it, Battles," Diamond said. "As we heard it, you know where a nice pot of money is staked out. You got away with thirty thousand dollars in that job you were sent up for. Nobody knows what happened to that money. Nobody but you. That's why they didn't hang you."

Matt laughed and stretched out on his own bed of leaves. "So that's it. You offer to cut me in on ten or twenty thousand dollars' ransom money— which you haven't got. And I'm to split up thirty thousand in appreciation."

Diamond smiled. "Then you *do* have that chunk of dough cached?"

"Even if I did, it still isn't enough to cut up four ways. There'd be nothing left worthwhile for anybody."

Diamond didn't speak for a long time. Matt,

disappointed, closed his eyes and began to give in to great weariness. He had been hoping to bait Diamond into some tangible information in the one matter he was interested in, above all. The train robbery.

Diamond spoke, as though having debated it and having reached a decision. "What if Turk and myself sweetened the pot with some sugar of our own?"

Matt came fully, vividly awake. But he managed to speak drowsily, without interest. "Yeah? What kind of sugar?"

"Yellow stuff. Gold. And plenty of it. Lots more than the grab you made at a country store."

"Keep talking," Matt said. "I'm trying to listen."

"Some other time," Diamond said. He added, "I hear that you're real swift with a gun, Battles."

"Do you believe everything you hear?"

"You made a rep down in Wyoming as a man to steer clear of. If the three of us stick together, we might be able to swing this thing from all angles. Maybe even the Rossiter end of it, although I admit that might not be worth the risk. We could go south with a real stake. But, right now, we're a long way from being out of the woods. The law won't quit soon on this one. We've got our work cut out to shake them off. Three heads are better than one. And three fast guns."

"Three?" Matt inquired. "Didn't I hear Shagrue say it was to be a four-way split?"

Diamond flashed his cold smile. "You heard wrong. There are only the three of us in on this. Turk, yourself and me."

His meaning was clear. The man who had engineered their escape and provided them with guns, food and the boat, was not included in Diamond's plans. No doubt he was slated for elimination in the same way Frank Welton had been erased.

Going farther along that line of reasoning, it was easy to believe that Diamond intended to limit the number to even less than three. To two. Shagrue and himself.

Or, more likely, to one. Himself.

CHAPTER ELEVEN

They remained in their hiding place until the third night, tortured by insects, sweltering in the humid heat of the marsh during the day. Clouds gathered at sunset of the third day. No rain came, but heat lightning played over the mountains to the west.

The river was dark as pitch and Diamond decided they'd never have a better chance of making it past Stone Lodge. He was right. They drifted undiscovered past the lights of the town at midnight and were camped in hiding ten miles downstream before dawn.

Three days later they were camped in wild, brushy country near where the Buffalo River joined the Missouri. Once again they were beset by mosquitoes, buffalo gnats and deer flies, and by the maddening, tiny no-seeums that choked and gagged them when they breathed.

Shagrue, tortured beyond endurance, burst into frenzied, arm-waving profanity as he fought the pests. Diamond, who seemed as indifferent to the insects as to heat and hardships, awakened. He had a six-shooter in his hand, and his eyes were deadly. "Shut up!" he raged. "Somebody might be poking around near here and could have heard that yowling!"

Shagrue quieted instantly. Diamond sat waiting and listening for any rumor of danger. After a long time he settled back and was almost instantly asleep.

Shagrue sat gazing at the sleeper, dread in his tough face. And bewilderment. Matt could see that Shagrue's slow mind was trying to grasp a new, terrible thought, trying to convince himself that the dark shadow that had suddenly passed over him had been only that—a shadow.

It had occurred to Shagrue that Diamond did not intend to share any part of the spoils with anyone, and with Turk Shagrue least of all.

Shagrue was not the only one over whom the black shadow lay. Matt had felt its increasing chill with each passing day, with each mile of the journey. Nancy gave him a glance and he saw the same somber fear there. The only question was of time and place. When would it come?

Diamond slept peacefully. For the time being, at least, he needed them. Nancy's value as a hostage, Matt's knowledge of a supposed cache of money, Shagrue's rawhide strength and shooting skill were factors that protected them from bullets in the back. Even these safeguards were frail and subject to Diamond's unpredictable moods.

Matt brushed at insects. His hands were swollen from the stabbing bites of the pests. So was his face. Nancy huddled forlornly on crossed legs, covering her head with her arms in an attempt to make herself as small as possible under the torture.

Matt touched her shoulder and said, "Into the river. They can't go under water at least."

She nodded. "It might help. I'll go crazy if this keeps up much longer."

They waded into shallow water alongside the skiff and found positions where they sat with the river to their chins, leaning their heads back against the dank planks of the craft. Her hair floated around them and helped give additional protection from the pests.

Presently she murmured, "He intends to get rid of us. All of us."

"Not until we're no longer valuable to him," Matt said.

"When will that be?"

"No telling. I'll know in time. I'll see that you get away."

"Why not now? Why wait? Why not tonight?"

"You'd never make it," he said.

"Maybe I'm tougher than you suspect."

"I know how tough you are. I still carry a few scars from rocks that a certain Miss Smarty Pants bounced off my skull a long time ago. But this isn't the Butte Creek school, and the people in this part of the world aren't school kids."

"You act like you're acquainted around here."

Matt shrugged. "A friend of mine and myself

got curious about this range a few years back and took a ride through it. Just for the hell of it. Ever hear of the Purgatory country?"

"Of course."

"You're in it right now. We didn't like what we saw that first time and got out. Strangers weren't welcome then and I don't imagine it's changed any. What few ranches there are around here are hangouts for thieves and wanted men and way stations for rustled cattle and stolen horses that are run back and forth in both Canada and the States. The Canadian line isn't far north of here. Some of the cusses who hang out in Purgatory were buffalo hunters in the old days. Some were trappers. All are bad. When a law officer comes into this part of the world he never comes alone. But the law doesn't come in very often. It's wasted time. They hardly ever find the man they want. The people in Purgatory live like gypsies, never staying long in one hangout."

"I see," she said. But she didn't seem impressed.

"They'd pick you up before you'd gone half a dozen miles," Matt said. "Likely the only thing that's saved you up to now is that there are three men with you."

She stared. "What do you mean?"

"Women are mighty scarce in Purgatory."

"Are you trying to say they already know we're here?"

"I'd bet on it."

She was silent for a time. "Even so, maybe I'd be better off," she finally said.

"Nothing could be worse than that for a woman."

She dropped her voice to a mere murmur. "This—this friend of yours who rode into Purgatory with you, was Johnny the Kid, perhaps?"

Matt frowned, warning her against risking any further mention of that name. But she persisted, speaking only in the faintest whisper. "I know all about my father arranging that fake holdup at Cyrus Johnson's store."

She had expected to startle him. She was surprised when Matt only nodded.

"You *knew* that I had been told?" she breathed.

"Yes. You're the only one who knows, outside of myself."

"Dad told you that I—?"

"I insisted on knowing." Matt peered at her. "You mean he didn't let you know he'd told me about you?"

"No." She was silent for a time. She eyed him, frowning. "I see now why you're so anxious that I stay alive. I'm very valuable to you, as well as to Diamond."

"That's right," Matt said.

She pursed her lips, glaring at him resentfully. "And all the time I thought—" she began.

Then she turned her back on him pretending that she wanted to fall asleep.

Shagrue spoke irritably from where he was trying to sleep. "What's goin' on there? What are you two palaverin' about?"

She turned and slapped Matt with all her strength. "If you try to touch me again I'll scratch out your eyes, you beast!" she said. "I mean it."

Matt's cheek burned from the force of the slap. She had meant it when she had delivered that blow.

Shagrue laughed jeeringly. "Seems like the lady don't cotton to you no more'n to me, Battles," he said.

Diamond awakened. He lifted his head and gazed at Matt and Nancy for a moment or two unsmilingly and with cold speculation.

He lay back and closed his eyes again. "There's to be no more talk that all of us don't hear," he said. "By anybody. And particularly by you, Battles, and the petticoat."

Nancy tilted her nose at Matt with an indignant toss of her head. But he saw a small twinkle of satisfaction deep in her eyes. His cheek still stung from the slap.

It came to him that although she was fully aware that her life meant little or nothing to Diamond she had the strength of will to push that knowledge into the background, knowing that her chances of escape were bettered by facing the situation and maintaining a calm front. For he was certain in his mind that she believed she

190

could get out of this country alive, in spite of his warning, and that she intended to try to escape at first chance.

There were even times when he suspected her of gaining strength from her situation. It was as though her nature fed on danger and that she was equipped to meet the challenge with a power of spirit that could not be conquered.

He discovered she was watching him from the corner of an eye. She seemed pleased with whatever she had seen in his face, and turned away again, and this time she seemed to fall asleep almost at once.

The high tension that had buoyed him also suddenly slacked away. He slept too, even in this unusual bed.

They set out again at twilight and a new moon was still in the sky when they entered the main river—the powerful Missouri.

They swung to the north side of the river. The going was easy for the most part as they took advantage of the current, but there were stretches where the river exacted toll—mudbanks in which they floundered and eddies that carried them into tangles of driftwood that wrapped clammy tentacles around them and from which they escaped only by sheer muscle, often carrying the skiff over obstructions.

At midnight they were all wading in ankle-deep

water to lighten the craft over a shallow stretch of water-covered sand that glittered with fool's gold in the starlight.

Even Nancy was adding her strength to the task, although previously she had defied Diamond's wrath by refusing to do anything that would help them.

Matt, straining to propel the boat over the shallows, suddenly realized that the water was not ankle-deep, but thigh-deep. Nancy, who was within arm's reach ahead, was also sinking in the river.

Yet, around them, he saw the shimmer of the surface of the sand, still barely covered by its glasslike coating of water.

"Quicksand!" he exclaimed. "Hang onto the boat or you'll go under!"

Diamond, on the opposite side of the craft, was nearly waist-deep, so suddenly had they floundered into the trap. Matt, too, was down to his hips. He felt the horror of the depths that would have engulfed him, but for the skiff.

The skiff was their salvation. Both he and Nancy grasped its combing and began fighting their way clear. Diamond, too, was escaping.

But Shagrue, who had been near the stern, heaving the skiff ahead with his oxlike strength, uttered a terrified shout.

"I'm sinkin'! Help me! In God's name, give me a hand!"

Shagrue had lost contact with the skiff. He was little more than half a dozen feet away, but was already down to his waist in the sand and sinking fast.

Matt could see his eyes shining with terror in the starlight. The eyes of a corpse.

"Doc!" Shagrue's voice was thin, unreal. And without hope. For Shagrue did not really expect Diamond, or anyone, to help him.

Diamond could have reached the sinking man. He was in the best position to make the try. It would have been a risk, for he would have had to leave the security of the skiff, lay flat on the sand so as to distribute his weight in order to reach Shagrue. He would be taking the chance that he would not mire down. And he would be gambling that both he and Shagrue would be pulled back to safety by Matt.

The risks were really not great, but Diamond did not take the gamble. He pulled himself, panting, over the side of the skiff and collapsed on the craft's bottom.

Matt wriggled free of the sand and into the craft. He caught Nancy by the shoulders and dragged her to safety.

During those seconds Shagrue's screaming was in his ears. He raced to the stern, stepping over Diamond and slid overside, flattening out on the surface.

Shagrue was down to his armpits. He quit

screaming when Matt reached for his hand. It was Shagrue's fingers that closed with frenzied strength on Matt's wrist.

They remained there for straining seconds. Matt's strength prevented Shagrue from sinking deeper, but he was not able to move him closer to the skiff.

"Right back of you!" Nancy spoke. "Grab the oar!"

Standing in the boat, she was extending an oar within Matt's reach.

"The skiff's almost afloat," she said. "We can move it alongside him."

Their churning had loosened the viscous sand so that she and Matt were able to move the skiff alongside Shagrue. She helped pull, first Matt, then Shagrue, from the sand. That took time and great effort. They all collapsed in the boat, limp and spent.

Diamond had offered no help. He eyed them coldly. "If there are any posses camped around here they'll be down on us before daybreak, with all that commotion going on."

They worked the skiff clear of the treacherous area. Shagrue was silent. Evidently there was no gratitude in him, no spark of appreciation for what Matt and Nancy had done. On the contrary, Matt sensed that Shagrue rather held him in scorn for having saved his life. In Shagrue's code, Matt had missed a chance to get rid of a man with whom he might have to share the robbery loot.

Matt found a moment to speak to Shagrue alone after they had made another of their hidden camps at dawn. "She should have left both of us in the sand, Shagrue," he said. "She knows you're not fit to live in the same world with her, but she had mercy on you. And on me. Keep that in mind, if you've got any wrong ideas about her. I'll stamp you out like I would any other spider, if you make a mistake."

Shagrue looked at him, looked at the six-shooter at his side and walked away without answering.

They ate the last of their food before setting out again at dusk. They had entered a section of the river where rocky bluffs, fringed by scrub cedar, looked down on them. The Missouri was narrow and swift, with the going dangerous even close to shore.

"How much farther?" Matt asked.

"This is the last stretch," Diamond said. "We're about through with this damned river. By tomorrow night there'll be horses to ride."

His voice lifted a little. "We've about made it into the clear. It'll be downhill from now on."

They were all gaunt, insect-bitten, and ragged in clothes that had been repeatedly soaked and dried on their bodies.

"Made it to where?" Matt asked.

"It wouldn't do you any good to know that, even

if I bothered to tell you," Diamond answered.

The night was half over when Diamond, who was taking a turn at the oars, along with Shagrue, paused and pointed to a tall, thin rock spire that stood like a steeple against the stars on the bluffs north of the river.

"We're there!" he exclaimed. "Church Rock, just like he described it! There can't be any mistake!"

He suddenly became voluble, bubbling with excitement. His icy outward demeanor was shattered. "By God, we made it!" he chattered exultantly. "We made it. Through hell and high water! Head for shore, Turk. We'll land anywhere we can find a good place."

Nancy aroused from the apathy she had adopted to shield herself from the hardships—and from thinking. No chance for an attempt to escape had presented itself during the river journey, but Matt guessed that the hope had flamed in her that an opportunity might come once they were on dry land.

Shagrue gave a grunt of joy and also emerged from his weary, mechanical routine at the oars. He began rowing with inspired strength.

The river's dark surface merged with the deep shadows of the bluffs. Presently Diamond picked out a feasible landing place on water-worn boulders. They swung in and Matt leaped ashore and steadied the skiff so that Nancy could land.

"Sink the skiff," Diamond said. "We won't need the cursed thing any more and I don't want anybody to find it."

He and Shagrue smashed holes in the hull with rocks, then weighted the boat down with more rocks and pushed it into deeper water where it sank from sight.

They left the river, laboriously climbing a slanting, brushy ascent until they reached the top of a bluff. The steeple-shaped butte came in sight again.

Diamond used this as a guidepoint. "It'll be a couple or three miles," he said. He spoke to Nancy, "As for you, my lady, don't get any ideas of trying to quit us. Even the coyotes have hydrophobia here in Purgatory at this time of year. There's a rattlesnake living in every prairie dog hole."

He added, "Not to mention the humans you're more likely to run into. A lot of the denizens of this country would give their hope of heaven—if they had such—to get their hands on a pretty girl like you."

"So I've been told," she said.

"Told? Who told you?" But Diamond had already guessed the answer. He peered close at Matt in the darkness. "You?" he asked. "You've been here before? In the Purgatory?"

"Yes." Matt offered nothing further.

Diamond was scowling, not liking Matt's

failure to offer information. "Do you know anybody in the Purgatory?" he finally asked.

"Maybe," Matt said. "Do you?"

Diamond suddenly laughed. "One thing I like about you, Battles, is that you don't give an inch."

"What else do you like about me?"

"I'll let you know if I find anything," Diamond said.

Matt let the matter drop. Always, he and Diamond came to sword points. Someday, no doubt, it must go farther than that.

They worked their way wearily through rocks and brush. Then they reached better going. Matt saw that they were following a dim wagon trail.

Presently the fresher scent of green grass overcame the resinous smell of cedar and sagebrush. He felt the softer underfooting of a natural meadow. A horse blew somewhere at a distance and he heard the stir of others. And the sound of a running stream.

"Purgatory Creek," Diamond said. "It must be."

The ridgepole of a sagging log shack appeared against the stars ahead. Its mud and rock chimney leaned drunkenly and was braced with a cedar pole.

Diamond whistled. The sound caused a greater stir among the unseen horses in the meadow.

They waited. Matt saw that Diamond and

Shagrue had drawn their six-shooters. Now they cocked the weapons. The metallic sounds were startlingly loud in the silence.

Matt's hand closed on Nancy's arm. He was prepared to hurl her to the ground if shooting started. She sensed this and remained obedient to his will. He could feel her quivering.

The silence went on. And on. Even though he could hear no tangible sound, Matt sensed that there was movement and life inside the shack, and that eyes were studying them from back of the tattered gunnysacks that served as curtains at the windows.

Then a deep voice spoke. "It's all right, Baldy. It's them sure enough."

Matt had heard that voice before. And so had Nancy, for he felt her stiffen in surprise.

Diamond sighed. He carefully lowered the hammer of the six-shooter and thrust the gun back in his belt.

"It's about time you spoke up!" he said querulously. "We're coming in."

Light flared in the place as a match was touched to the wick of a lamp. The door opened and a beefy man stood outlined against the light.

"Who's with you, Ed?" Diamond asked.

"Baldy and one of the boys," the big man said.

The speaker was Ed Ledge, the captain of guards at Stone Lodge. But Matt did not share Nancy's surprise. He had been expecting it. Here was the fourth man with whom Diamond was supposed to share the train robbery bullion.

"One of the boys?" Diamond challenged sharply. "Who?"

Ledge turned his head and addressed someone inside the shack. "What's your name, fella? Your last name."

"Texas," an irritable voice answered. "Tex Texas is my handle. If your pal out there don't like it, I'll just naturally bog down an' cry."

"If I find out I don't like it, fellow," Diamond spoke, "you'll be the first to find it out."

Another voice, crusty, with more authority, spoke back of Ledge. "Tex is all right. Tell your pal to let him alone."

"Come on in, Doc," Ledge said hastily. "And you too, Shagrue. And—"

Ledge had left the doorway and was approaching them. He had discovered Nancy's presence. He halted and stood glaring. He whirled on Diamond, his voice suddenly ugly. "What'd you bring *her* here fer?"

"Any reason why not?" Diamond asked silkily.

"Dammit, Doc, she'll blab too much. Baldy won't like this."

"Baldy *don't* like it," the crusty voice spoke. A man came from the shack, still stuffing a shirt into his belt. He was short and barrel-shaped with powerful bowed legs. He had a cap and ball pistol slung over his shoulder by its holster belt.

200

Baldy strode among them. He was unwashed, unshaven. He pushed a bearded, ugly face within inches of Nancy. "She's a young 'un at least," he said. "A mighty purty squaw."

He turned on Diamond. "What yuh aim to do with her?"

"She's going with us," Diamond said.

Ledge spoke. "Now why—?"

"For the same reason we took her with us off the Hill," Diamond snapped. "She stops bullets."

There was a silence. Diamond spoke again. "That closes the subject. This is a hell of a way to treat guests. I need a bath and a shave. I smell almost as ripe as you, Baldy, and that's enough to sicken a skunk."

Baldy took that as a compliment, and guffawed. "Hell, Doc, you know that water weakens a man. Whisky's the only thing fit for a human bein'."

"Speaking of whisky, I could use a drink," Diamond said. "Four fingers. And then a second one the same size."

"Me too," Shagrue spoke.

They entered the shack. The place was larger than it had seemed from the outside. There were half a dozen bunks in upper and lower tiers along the two walls. Rude benches sat beside a table which had cracked black oilcoth as a cover and bore a worn deck of cards and scattered chips.

An opening led to a kitchen that was excavated

into the side of a rise of ground against which the shack was built.

A sullen, scowling man sat on a bunk, looking them over. He was rail-thin with thin, stringy hair and a three-day stubble of beard. He had on saddle breeches and a shirt, but his boots were off, and his toes poked through holes in his socks. In one item, his attire was complete. He had on a well-oiled cartridge belt and a good holster with a six-shooter nested there which had a fine pearl handle.

Diamond inspected him with deliberate distaste. "Are you Tex Texas?" he asked.

"I ain't Buffalo Bill," the man said. He was an outlaw, of course. Men like Tex Texas, which was not his real name, Matt knew, could get rest and food and fresh horses—if they had the price—at ranches such as this in the Purgatory. And the price was always high.

CHAPTER TWELVE

Baldy adjusted the smoking wick of the lamp so that the best of its light fell on Matt and Nancy. They endured his suspicious appraisal. Nobody spoke for a time.

Baldy particularly took his time inspecting Matt from head to foot, rubbing a grimy hand meditatively across his hairless pate while he seemed to be racking his mind for some thought that was eluding him.

"Where've I seen you before, fella?" he asked.

Matt had released Nancy's arm, but he discovered now that she was clinging to his hand. Her fingers were locked tightly. He felt them grow even tighter. He guessed that she was praying inwardly that Baldy, if he really had seen Matt in the past, would not remember when or where. And above all, would not link his name with that of Johnny the Kid.

"I couldn't say," Matt said. "I've been places, seen things. Likely we crossed trails somewhere."

Baldy shrugged. "I reckon not. I never forget a face." He grinned and added, "It don't pay in my business."

The moment of tension passed. Matt felt Nancy's fingers relax and heard her sigh a little. Matt surmised that it had been Baldy's method of tricking men into revealing any flaws in their reasons for being at his hangout.

Baldy poked the ashes in the stove alive and added fresh fuel. "I'll boil some kawfee," he said.

Tex Texas was staring at Nancy. "There's one thing I never cotton to," he said, "an' that's stealin' women."

Diamond turned on him. "You've done worse things, I take it."

"Never mind what I've done, mister. It's the law dogs I'm thinkin' about. When a woman is stole, they never give up. You'll bring a posse down on us."

"You're always free to dust out," Baldy snapped.

"That's just what I'm doin'," the man said. "The best they do is to string you up for these kind o' capers. The worst they do is plenty."

He pulled on his boots, dragged his saddlebags from beneath the bunk and began stuffing his meager belongings into them and rolling his bedding.

"You're not leaving just yet," Diamond said.

Tex Texas looked at him. "No? Why not?"

"It's not because we like your company," Diamond said. "But you might talk. To the wrong people."

Tex Texas laughed disdainfully. "Now who would I talk to, a sheriff?"

"Maybe," Diamond said.

Tex Texas stamped his feet tight in his boots, slung his belongings over his shoulder and headed for the door.

"I told you that you were staying here," Diamond said.

"You got any notion you can stop me?" Tex Texas asked. He was younger than Matt had estimated at first. He could be no more than much beyond voting age. But he was sure of himself, sure of his skill with the pearl-handled six-shooter.

"Yes," Diamond said. "I can stop you. And will."

Tex Texas laughed again, a forced effort. He continued to move toward the door, but kept an eye on Diamond, his hand near his holster.

"Hold it, you fool!" Baldy screeched. "Wait, Doc! Don't blood up my place. Don't—"

Matt caught Nancy around the waist, and dove with her to cover beyond the line of bunks.

The killing came with the winking violence of a lightning flash and the crash of gun thunder. Tex Texas went for his .45, but Diamond was faster. His bullet tore through the lean man's throat.

Tex Texas fired one shot, but the slug only brought down a shower of dust from the roof. Dying, he staggered, choking on his own blood. He tried to bring his dazed eyes into focus, tried to sight his weapon again.

Diamond fired a second shot with deliberation.

The same way he had shot Frank Welton. It was the *coup de grâce* bullet that made certain there would never be retaliation, from the victim at least. It sent Tex Texas toppling backward through the open door. He fell dead in the yard.

Powdersmoke fogged the shack. Nancy lay with her face buried in her arms. "Stay there," Matt said. "Don't look. It's over, but it's nothing for you to see."

She complied. Matt got to his feet. Baldy and Ledge and Shagrue, who had also dived to cover, were appearing also.

Baldy said querulously, "Dammit, Doc, look at that mess I've got to muck up. I asked you not to start any shootin' inside the house."

"Who was he?" Matt asked. "What was his real name?"

"How would I know?" Baldy snarled. "I don't ask 'em to give me their life histories."

He added, still complainingly, "An' what'll we do with him now?"

"Take him down to the river and dump him in," Diamond said. "It wouldn't be the first one. Or bury him with a posy on his chest, for all I give a damn. I don't give a whoop what you do with him. But drag him out of my sight. I need some sleep."

Baldy and Turk Shagrue dragged the dead man away by the heels through the dust toward a

206

rickety shed where a wagon was sheltered from the weather.

Diamond closed the door. Nancy arose, and Diamond paused, gazing at her speculatively for a time as though weighing some sudden thought in his mind.

Matt went ice-cool, bracing himself, ready to draw. There had been only a time or two previously when he had set himself this way— ready to meet the greatest issue a human being can face. One of those supreme moments had been the day in Wyoming when he and Johnny Kidd had stood in the sun facing six paid gunfighters.

Diamond had once more slain a man. And he was still in a killing mood. Matt was sure that he was debating whether this was not as good a time as any to put an end to Nancy whose testimony would certainly send him to the gallows if she ever faced him in a court.

But the moment passed. Diamond decided, evidently, that she was still of value as a hostage. He pulled a blanket from a bunk and tossed it to her. "Sleep in the kitchen," he said. "And see that you stay there."

The harsh quiver of released nerve strain ran through Matt. Once more the showdown with Diamond had been put off.

Nancy was ashen, all the sureness battered out of her. She knew how thin had been the margin of her respite from Diamond's intention to silence her permanently. She looked at Matt, waiting for his advice. He nodded and she fled into the dugout with the blanket.

There was no door to shield her from observation. It was an effective prison, however, for the only way of escape would be through the main room of the shack.

Matt doused his head in cold water from a pail on the wash bench outside. He ran his hand over his lengthening stubble of beard, then entered the shack, pulled off his boots and rolled into one of the bunks.

Diamond and Ledge were sitting in the far corner, their heads together, talking in whispers. Evidently there was fierce difference of opinion between them. Matt knew that he and Nancy were the subjects of the discussion and he guessed that Ledge was demanding that Diamond get rid of at least Nancy immediately.

Baldy and Shagrue returned from disposing of Tex Texas's body. They took long, deep pulls from Baldy's whisky jug and made a few callous jests about being haunted before they turned in.

They were soon asleep. Tex Texas's body had been fed to the fish in the Missouri River, and they were already forgetting even the false name under which he had lived.

Ledge also climbed into a bunk, but Diamond, apparently tireless as usual, was still awake, sitting staring at nothing, chewing a cigar that Baldy had given him, when Matt fell asleep. Thinking. Planning.

And it was Diamond's hand that awakened him. The sun was already beating down on the shack. "Do your sleeping wintertime," Diamond said. "Or in your old age if you live that long."

He added, "If you need some Dutch courage, try some of Baldy's rotgut. He stills it himself. Any that's left over, he uses as wolf poison."

Matt looked around. "Where's the Chisholm girl?"

Diamond jerked a thumb toward the open door. "Out there."

"What?"

"Keep your hair on. A lady's entitled to privacy when she takes a bath."

"You let her go out there alone?" Matt demanded angrily.

He headed for the door, seizing his boots, but Diamond halted him. "She didn't want company."

"She's probably a mile away already and—" Matt began.

"Not likely. Not without shoes in this country. Not without clothes."

Matt's expression caused Diamond to laugh. "She *has* got a blanket. She'll be back." He added, "For one thing, she can't go a hundred yards out of that brush without us sighting her, and she knows it."

He pointed. "Here comes the lady now. And decently wrapped in her blanket after her bath. You can relax, Battles. She had sense enough not to try to desert us."

Nancy had appeared from the creek brush. She came slowly to the shack. Matt decided that she had fought a losing battle with herself. Reason had prevailed and she had reluctantly given up any thought of trying to escape with only a blanket to shield her.

She entered the shack, pale with humiliation. She did not glance at Matt. Ledge and Shagrue uttered guffaws. Shagrue attempted to snatch the blanket away as she passed by him on the way to the kitchen.

She seized a fork from the table and jabbed it into Shagrue's hand. He yelled with pain and anger and lurched from the bench, trying to seize her.

Matt moved in and caught Shagrue by his thick wiry hair, lifting him and jamming him against a wall. Shagrue launched a knee at Matt's stomach, but Matt had anticipated and evaded the attempt. He hit Shagrue twice, a right and a left.

Shagrue was tough, but those blows numbed him. Matt struck again, a right to the body. Shagrue remained pinned to the wall for an instant, then slipped to the floor and sagged over on his side, glassy-eyed.

Nancy wrapped the blanket tighter around her. "I only wish I could have done that," she said. She walked on into the dugout.

Diamond arose, lifted a tincup of rotgut and made a mocking bow over Shagrue's dazed form. "Rest in peace," he said. He looked at Matt. "You pack a wallop, Battles," he said with grudging respect.

Baldy sloshed water over Shagrue. The man finally got to his feet, green around the mouth. He looked at Diamond, expecting support.

Diamond only eyed him coldly. "You fool," he said. "You got what you deserved. The next time I'll take a hand in it myself. I told you before that the world's full of women and that I don't want any trouble over this one."

Shagrue had to accept that. He walked shakily out to the wash bench and treated his bruised face. He did not look at Matt when he returned, but it was evident that his grudge was deep and deadly.

Diamond spoke to Baldy. "Better slope out and see if your horses are all right."

Baldy scowled, realizing that he was being dismissed from his own house, but he finally sullenly tramped out.

"Now we can talk," Diamond said. "You've had enough to drink, Ledge. Put down that cursed jug. You too, Turk. And I don't want any more fighting. Any scores you have to settle

211

will be taken care of afterward. We've got more important things to think about."

He added, "We're pulling out of here tonight."

"Where are we heading?" Matt asked.

"We'll be across the line by tomorrow night."

"Canada? Why go there?"

"Only temporarily. We'll travel east, then swing back to this side of the border."

"It don't pay to fool with the Mounties," Ledge grumbled.

"The Mounties are spread mighty thin in this part of the country," Diamond said impatiently. "But it's a little bit different on this side of the line. Baldy says that posses are still swarming, hunting us. One bunch of manhunters searched this place, but luckily it was two days ago. They may come back."

"The border won't stop them from dogging us if they cut our sign," Shagrue said from puffed lips. "They'll follow us into Canada. To hell, if need be. It's the girl they're hunting. I wish to God you'd never thought of takin' her with us, Doc."

Diamond glared at him with contempt. "She kept the bullets away from us before. She can do it again. And they've got to find us, first. That won't be easy. Everything will be taken care of. Baldy isn't the only rascal who likes to pick up some easy money by helping people like us. There are some like him on the other side of the line. He knows where to find them. They'll hide us, if need be, and furnish us with fresh horses."

"You ain't sayin' that Baldy's goin' with us?" Ledge demanded, alarmed.

"Only as long as he's needed to show us the way," Diamond said. "He doesn't know anything more than what I've told him. Which is nothing. He knows better than to ask questions. We'll cut loose from him after we're in the clear."

Shagrue spoke. "He ain't doin' this for nothin', now is he? Not if I know Baldy."

"Hardly," Diamond said. "Help like this comes high."

"How much?" Ledge demanded.

"Baldy says a thousand will take care of everything," Diamond said.

"A thousand dollars!" Ledge squealed. "Why the thievin'—!"

"It's worth it," Diamond snapped. "And the deal is closed. We'll pay his price, and in cash. We're in enough trouble without getting Baldy and his outfit after us. I'd rather be caught by a posse than his friends."

"Where do we get the money?" Matt asked. "This thousand dollars."

Diamond smiled blandly. "From safes in mercantile stores, perhaps. Or from under rocks."

Matt's brows arched in mock puzzlement. "I don't follow you."

"I'm sure you do. I'm also sure you're way ahead of me, my friend. But Turk here is a little slow. We'll travel east after we get across the line and keep going until we cut back into the States and travel south along the Rainbow Mountains until we're near a town named Rainbow. That's your home town, I believe, Battles?"

"That's where I used to hang up my spurs," Matt said.

Diamond's voice became brittle. "Exactly how close to Rainbow did you cache the money you got in that store holdup?"

Matt laughed jeeringly. "Now, even if I knew, why would I mention a thing like that here in public?"

"I tell you we can't double-cross people like Baldy," Diamond said. "I've told him we'd pay the thousand if he'd get us within reach of this town of Rainbow. I wouldn't like to disappoint him. It might be unlucky for all of us."

"I might be able to pay my own way," Matt said. "How about the rest of you?"

Diamond smiled almost admiringly. "You still don't give an inch, do you, Battles?"

"Not when money's concerned," Matt said. "And not just to be sociable."

"Look! We're all in this together. Hoofs to horns. I told you on the Hill that I'd match every dollar you put in the pot with two of mine."

"From that stagecoach holdup for which they

sent you and Shagrue to the Hill?" Matt asked ironically.

Diamond flushed. "That was chickenfeed. A mistake. We believed there was an express box aboard. There wasn't."

"So you picked the pockets of the passengers," Matt jeered. "Robbed even a woman, so I was told in the Lodge."

Shagrue, bristling, spoke angrily. "Ever hear o' the Cedar Springs train robbery about—?"

"Shut up!" Diamond exploded. But the interruption came too late and Diamond realized it. He glared at Shagrue with murderous anger. "You always talk too much, Turk," he said.

He looked at Matt and shrugged. "All right," he said. "The cat's out of the bag."

Matt rolled a cigarette, making an elaborate show of taking his time. Even so he spilled tobacco. He wanted a chance to settle down, ease the rush of wild excitement that had swept through him.

He made sure he had his voice under control before speaking again. After all these black months—ostracism and suspicion, of days and nights in dungeons, of pacing a cell, of frustration and doubt—he had at last touched the key that might unlock the truth about Johnny Kidd.

A key that he might not really want to turn.

"So the cat's out of the bag," he said.

"A fat cat," Diamond said.

Matt eyed Diamond derisively. "Are you trying to tell me that you were in on that train stickup at Cedar Springs? Sure, I remember hearing about it. They got away with quite a pile of stuff. Bar gold that was being shipped East by the bank at Rainbow."

"That's right," Diamond said. "Gold bullion. And plenty of it. We had to load it on our horses and walk afoot to get away with it."

"Now I'll tell a tall one," Matt jeered.

"You're hearing the truth," Diamond snapped.

Matt still pretended to be mockingly disbelieving. "That train holdup was pulled quite a while ago."

"About a year ago," Diamond said.

"Then how come they put you on the Hill for a measly thing like that stagecoach holdup?"

"Until now, nobody but ourselves knew we had been at Cedar Springs. We had to take Ledge into our confidence, so that he would help spring us out of the Lodge. He's to get an equal share."

Matt permitted his skepticism to fade a trifle. "So what?"

"We're willing to take you in on the same terms. Share and share alike."

"Just out of the goodness of our hearts?"

Diamond's sardonic smile appeared. "Not exactly. We need money to pay off Baldy. Cash."

"You've just been telling me you had enough gold to sull a horse or two."

"That's exactly the point. In the first place, it isn't cash. It's bar bullion. In the second place, and even more to the point, if Baldy ever got wind of what we're really shooting for, none of us would ever see South America. We'd never be able to shake off him or his pals."

"I'll keep on listening," Matt said.

"If you could come up with the thousand dollars to pay off Baldy, I figure he'd take it and pull out. He doesn't know about us being in on the Cedar Springs job. But he *does* know all about you sticking up that big mercantile at Rainbow and getting away with thirty thousand dollars."

"Maybe he's after that bunch of money," Matt said. "After all, that's a pretty big wad all by itself. At least I think so."

"That's possible, but I doubt it. In fact I've sort of planted the belief in his mind that you weren't in on that job alone, and there isn't too much of the thirty thousand left. I doubt if he figures it would be worth taking the risk."

Matt debated it. "Maybe you're right."

"I know I'm right," Diamond said.

Matt finally shrugged. "All right. I'll buy in. I'll ante up a thousand dollars to get rid of Baldy."

Even as he spoke, he was wondering if he was making a mistake that might undo everything he had accomplished. He did not have the remotest idea as to where or how he could get his hands on a thousand dollars. But there was no turning

217

back now. He had to bluff it through to the finish.

"But not a cent more until I see the color of your own gold, Diamond," he said. "How do I know you're not pulling the long bow about that train holdup?"

"You'll see the yellow stuff," Diamond said and clapped him on the back. "We'll throw the whole pot together for the split. Or maybe go partners and buy us a ranch down on the pampas. They say the cow hands down there throw a sort of a rope and ball affair instead of a lass rope. They call it a bolero. I'd like to see that done."

Diamond was being far too generous in offering to share the train loot. Matt thought of Frank Welton. And of Tex Texas. Life was cheap with him.

Shagrue picked up the whisky jug, sloshed the contents around and took a deep pull. "Glad that's settled," he said. "My gullet was dryer'n a railroad spike after all that palaver."

He took another pull from the jug, shuddered and wiped his thick lips.

Diamond gave him a look of disgust and said, "Finish the jug, if you can't keep away from it, and sleep it off, Turk. It's the last rotgut you'll get until we're entirely out of the woods, I'll promise you."

He added, "All of us will be ready to pull out at early dark, drunk or sober."

Matt glanced toward the kitchen. He was sure

Nancy had heard everything that had been said. Diamond's disregard of this was further proof that he had no intention of letting her live to use that knowledge.

"What about the girl?" Matt asked.

"I've already said she's going with us," Diamond said. "That stands. Got any better ideas?"

"Not right at the minute," Matt said. He looked at Diamond. "What about this idea of yours of shaking down the Rossiter outfit for money?"

Diamond shrugged. "I'm still thinking that over."

Ed Ledge spoke. "You can quit thinking, Doc. I'm dead ag'in it. It's too dangerous."

"I'll do the thinking," Diamond snapped.

But Matt knew that at least that part of Diamond's plan had been abandoned. Diamond, too, evidently had decided that an attempt to collect ransom was not worth the risk.

CHAPTER THIRTEEN

They resumed their journey at twilight, mounted on horses bearing brands that Matt was certain had been worked over by an expert. They carried food in their saddlebags, and this included a supply of pemmican.

Baldy said that the pemmican had been made by Blackfoot squaws in the old way, although beef had been used instead of buffalo meat. Rustled beef, no doubt. It had been cooked and dried in its own fat, pounded to shreds and mixed with wild cherries and herbs until it was almost as hard as leather. It formed a highly concentrated item of nourishment.

"It smells like a tannery," Diamond said. "Blast you, Baldy, is this the best you can do in the way of grub?"

"It'll smell like this here milk an' honey they talk about, if you have to hole up somewhere for a week or two while the posses try to run you down. It fills the belly, hot or cold."

Nancy rode ahead of Matt, her ankles lashed beneath the horse which she was riding astride.

"What if this beast spooks and tries to spill me?" she demanded. "This saddle might slip, and I'll be kicked to death."

"I'll shoot the horse, if need be," Matt said.

"How very, very comforting," she sniffed.

They must have covered forty or more miles that night. The only time Diamond spoke was toward daylight. "Baldy says we'll hole up until dark. We'll be in Canada by this time tomorrow night."

They slept during the day in a ravine that Baldy found and resumed the journey again at twilight. They were bearing directly on the North Star, traveling at a pace that tired the horses so that their heads were down and they could not be stirred out of a plodding gait.

The Big Dipper had swung around to the midnight position when Baldy passed the word that they were across the international border. They were on an open plain, and when they camped at dawn, Matt could see the enormity of this flat, rolling expanse. The buffalo grass, unmarred as yet by the plows of the farmers, stretched in all directions to the rims of the dawn sky. They camped in a shallow dry wash, and the four men took turns standing watch during the day. But no person could approach them on the plains without being sighted miles away.

They all awakened in the heat of the afternoon and chewed disconsolately on the tough pemmican, for Baldy would not permit the building of even a tiny fire.

"Smoke," he said. "Kin be seen a fur piece if the sun hits it right. An' it kin build a fire under us hotter'n the hinges o' Hades. There're other breaks in the plain, an' who knows but what a posse might be doin' jest what we're doin'. Waitin', an' restin'—an' lookin'.'"

But all that moved on the plain that day as far as the eye could see were prairie dogs and the wind. And the slow progress of the brassy sun.

Nancy nibbled at the tough pemmican. She had braided her hair in a tight plait and coiled it on her head. She had sat straight and defiant in the saddle during the long miles, unspeaking, but always alert for a chance to escape.

That chance came for the first time when they resumed their journey at dusk. The run of the trail caused them to string out, single file, while they were descending a steep cutbank into the floor of a sizable dry wash. She was out of sight of all the others for a moment, and she kicked her horse into motion, and headed down the wash in an attempt to flee into the gathering darkness.

But the bay she was riding was the slowest animal in the party. Diamond had seen to that. Matt spurred his horse into a gallop and overtook her without trouble. He caught the reins of the bay and dragged it to a stop.

Diamond had belatedly taken up the pursuit, but he slowed his horse to a trot when he saw that Matt had overtaken her.

"Don't try that again," Matt told her. "They'll only shoot you, or run you down and drag you back. The sign isn't right for a move like that."

"How much longer do you think I can stand this sort of thing?" she sobbed. "I'm not made of steel." She added, "Even if you are."

"What do you mean, me made of steel. I'm human too."

"You don't show it. You know that Diamond intends to kill you once he gets his hands on this money you're supposed to have hid somewhere."

" 'Supposed' to have hid? Do you mean you're actually beginning to believe I might be telling the truth about not having fallen for temptation that night in Rainbow?"

They were not able to talk any more at that moment, for Diamond now came within earshot. Diamond rode alongside, seized Nancy's arm and shook her roughly. "Don't make any more mistakes like that," he said. "One more will be your last."

However, at times, Matt found chances to exchange a few words with her when the others were out of hearing. This fragmentary conversation took place over a period of several days of cautious travel eastward.

They obtained new horses on the second night at a shabby ranchhouse, hidden in a brushy draw where a squawman and two hard-faced men who knew Baldy inspected them carefully and wisely, but asked no questions.

This was repeated later on at a hangout on a

stream where the only occupant was a huge, wild-eyed, bearded man who preached of righteousness and sneered at them and had a worn prayer book open on the greasy table at which they ate the food Baldy prepared for them.

They left the plain and entered broken hills where the going became too rough for travel in the darkness and they were forced to risk the open sunlight. In addition, they came upon the trail of half a dozen riders. The sign was less than a day old. They crossed the tracks later on the same day.

That jarred them out of their complacency. They had believed they were beyond pursuit, but these riders undoubtedly were manhunters who were ranging the country for sign of quarry. And that quarry was themselves.

Toward sundown they sighted riders far in the distance as they sat under cover of timber on a ridge. Among the group the sun marked out a red jacket. A mounted policeman was with the manhunters.

This drove them to tense cover for two days, during which Diamond and Ledge and Shagrue sat with guns in their hands while on watch, ready to settle it with gunpowder if the posse picked up their trail.

The posse failed to find them. After another day, they pushed ahead again. Diamond began to relax. "If they missed us back there it's hardly likely they'll swing much farther east," he said. "They're not even sure we came in this direction. It's onto two weeks since we busted out of the Lodge. They'll be giving up soon."

However, Diamond still did not take chances. He and Shagrue often scouted ahead to study their route for possible danger.

It was during one of their absences that Matt got his first chance to resume the conversation that had been interrupted days ago. Ledge and Baldy were sleeping, leaving him to guard Nancy alone.

"You heard me make that deal with Diamond," he said.

"Yes. I was listening."

"Then you know, at least, that I had nothing to do with the train holdup."

"Yes." She was silent for a time. "But—"

"But you don't know about Johnny," he said.

"There's the post card he sent you," she said reluctantly. "Dad told me about it. I knew Johnny when I was a child. I would never have believed he'd do anything like that. But—"

"But people change. Especially a person who is scarred and crippled by pulling a friend out of a range fire. That's what you're thinking, isn't it?"

"Why didn't Johnny come forward after the train holdup and say so if he had nothing to do with it? Why did he just drop out of sight? Dad told me he sent you that post card at least two weeks after the holdup."

She added, "Maybe it was a forgery."

"It was no forgery," Matt said tiredly. "Johnny wrote it. I feel sure of that."

He looked at her. "So you know I had no part in the train stickup. But how about the other job? Cyrus Johnson's murder. You still think I might have—"

"Bosh!" she exploded. "I never believed you did that."

He glared at her. "What? But you've acted like I was poison."

"That was for Diamond's benefit. He's been watching us far more closely than he pretends. He doesn't like the way you've stood up for me."

Matt nodded. "I know that too. I've got to work harder at making him believe I've fallen for you."

She gave him a slanting look. "I imagine that *is* rather trying. You're not a very good actor."

Matt grinned. "In addition to trying to hood-wink Diamond, I've got to be careful not to get too bold in another direction. I don't want to get belted again. Or maybe you'll bounce a rock off my head, like you used too, Miss Smarty Pants."

"I'd bounce one right now if I had a rock," she said. "I don't like that Smarty Pants name and you know it."

"You can mark one problem off the list, at least," Matt said. "Don't do any worrying about

Diamond trying to shake down your friend, Jeff Rossiter, for ransom. Diamond's got too many other irons in the fire to go ahead with anything like that."

"I hope so," she said. "It would be embarrassing."

"Embarrassing? That's a hell of a way to put it."

"Well, that's the way I put it, Mr. Bucko," she said, bridling.

"You can't believe that this Rossiter jigger would balk at paying the price."

"Of course not," she snapped. "I'm not exactly that worthless. It would be the only thing any decent man could do. But, under the circumstances, I'd rather die than have to ask Jeff Rossiter to bail me out of this fix."

Matt eyed her. "Under what circumstances?"

"That," she said, "is none of your concern."

"What do you mean, none of my concern? My God, here we are, both of us likely to get our heads blown off by Diamond and you act like that."

"I don't see what being here has anything to do with my private affairs."

"Private affairs? So that's it? You and Rossiter had a falling out. Right?"

She glared at him. "You certainly are a Jack Pry if I ever met one. If you *must* know, Mr. Rossiter asked me to marry him. I told him, as politely as possible, that I could never be more than a good friend to him."

"A good friend! I bet that graveled him."

"Well, he wasn't exactly happy about it," she said, and had to giggle. "In fact he acted like a bear with a sore paw. He seemed to think he was the prize catch of the year and that I was out of my mind."

"What's wrong with him?" Matt asked. "He seemed to stack up as a well-turned-out dude, even if he was too old for you."

"He has two subjects of conversation," she said. "First, there's himself. Secondly, the matter of prize cattle and the breeding thereof. He doesn't like to be interrupted, particularly when involved in discussing subject number one. The truth is, he's a cussed bore. What he needs is a wife who's deaf and dumb."

"Well, well!" Matt said. "You're certainly not either of those things."

Somehow, the day seemed brighter suddenly. At that moment, Diamond and Shagrue returned, bringing word they believed it was safe to proceed. He and Nancy did not have a chance to talk again until the next day.

When the opportunity came, she resumed the conversation as though it had not been interrupted, while they followed a twisting route through a maze of small buttes and dry stream beds.

"You still suspect, deep inside you, that it could have been my father who killed Mr. Johnson," she said, "and that he couldn't resist taking the money when he knew that he had a perfect way out by putting the blame on you."

Matt nodded. "But it never did ring quite true."

"Nor did it ring true with him that you were guilty," she said. "But he couldn't figure out the answer."

"One thing's for sure," Matt said. "*Somebody* must have known that my going there was a frameup. Your father must have confided in someone we didn't know about."

"Or Cyrus Johnson might have done it," she said.

Matt nodded. "That's possible too. Whoever that person is, he's the one who killed Cy Johnson and cleaned out the safe."

He added, "And he's the one who tried to kill your father in the street that morning, and then took a shot at me. He wanted to wipe out everybody who knew it was a frameup."

"Why didn't you tell the judge and jury that my father had talked you into going through with a fake holdup?"

"Johnny the Kid," Matt said tersely.

She eyed him critically. "Does loyalty to a friend have to go that far?"

"He went the whole route to pull my bacon out of the fire. Furthermore, right at that time, I felt that when it came down to cases it would be easy to prove I didn't kill Cy Johnson."

He added wryly, "I couldn't have been more wrong, especially now that your father's gone. I had banked on him standing by me when I asked for a new hearing. All he had to do was to testify that he was the one who had thought up the scheme."

"You've still got a witness who can testify to that. Me."

Their talk had been unduly long and Matt motioned a warning for caution. "I still can't prove that temptation didn't overcome me," he murmured, and moved farther away.

Ledge had twisted in the saddle and was peering suspiciously at them from bloodshot eyes.

Matt gave him a scowl. "Didn't anybody ever tell you not to eavesdrop when a fellow was trying to make talk with a pretty girl?"

But Ledge, although he said nothing, was not entirely satisfied by that, and kept close to them as much as possible, so it was some time before there was another chance for conversation.

They veered south. Diamond was now so confident they had shaken off pursuit that he and Shagrue rode into a little settlement and returned with a fresh supply of food. It was Ledge who had grudgingly supplied the small amount of cash that was needed for the purchases.

"It seems to me," Ledge said, "that I'm the

king pin in this deal. I got you all out of the Lodge, an' now I'm putting up the money for the whole operation. Maybe we better start thinkin' of cuttin' me in for a bigger slice o' the pie than just a quarter of it."

"I'll do the thinking," Diamond said.

Ledge opened his mouth to pursue the subject, then took a second look at Diamond and went silent. He did not mention the matter again.

They were traveling again at night. They recrossed the border out of Canada and crossed the Dakota Pacific track at a point not far west of Cedar Springs. Another of Baldy's shady ranching friends guided them to a spot where their horses forded the Missouri River in knee-deep water.

"This train holdup," Matt said, "was pulled about thirty miles east of Cedar Springs, as I recall it. That's only about two days' ride from here."

"You recall a lot, don't you?" Diamond said.

"Every cowboy in the Rainbow country put in his spare time whenever he was within miles of that place hunting for the bullion cache," Matt said. "Including me."

"You didn't find it, did you?" Diamond said and laughed. "It's farther than thirty miles east of the town. That's why." He added, "If you're trying to prod me into lifting the bullion first, it won't work. What would we do with Baldy? I tell you the only way is for you to produce the thousand dollars. And Rainbow is a lot closer than the bullion."

They camped the next dawn in thick brush along a stream less than ten miles from Rainbow. They could see the faint haze of the morning chimney smoke of the community rising above the ridges to the south.

Tension and nerve strain was having its way, now that they were nearing their objectives in the desperate journey they had made. Ledge and Shagrue had been increasingly at sword's point, each taking offense at trivialities.

Shagrue, whose turn it was to act as cook, was ladling boiling-hot stew from their smoke-blackened kettle onto the tin plates they held. He deliberately spilled some of the liquid on Ledge's hand.

Ledge, with a howl of pain, hurled the contents of the plate into Shagrue's face. Then they were at each other, fists swinging, shoes kicking, thumbs hooking for eye gouges. They were frenzied, maddened, locked in a senseless, brutal, no-quarter combat.

Diamond made no move to interfere. He disdainfully moved farther away and sat on a rock, eating with his customary fastidiousness while he watched the battle with detached interest.

Baldy also remained apart and neutral. Matt

looked at Nancy. There was horror in her, and an appeal. She was asking him to intervene. But he refused. He was certain that to do so would shatter the restraint that held them all by a thin thread and the result would be a general battle.

The same horror gripped him as he watched. This was a battle to the death. And Ledge was losing. He was soft and far overweight. He was gasping. His face had a greenish hue.

Suddenly he collapsed. He reeled and fell flat on his face, clutching at his chest, wheezing for air. Shagrue leaped at him, brogans first, to continue the ferocious punishment.

Diamond spoke. "Never mind, Turk! I think his light went out, from the looks. I always figured that he had a bad heart. Let me take a peek."

Shagrue abruptly retreated, all the fury ebbing out of him as he stared. Diamond leisurely put his plate aside, walked to where Ledge lay and turned his body over with the toe of his shoe.

He dropped to one knee and briefly examined the big man. Ledge's wheezing breathing had ceased. Diamond looked up at Shagrue. "He's dead," he said. "Too much exertion."

Nancy dropped the plate she had been holding. She turned abruptly and fled away from the camp into the brush.

Matt followed her. The refrain of an old childhood rhyme ran through his head. And now there were three. Diamond, Shagrue, and himself.

Baldy didn't count. Baldy was only waiting for his pay for furnishing them with horses.

Nancy halted at a distance and stood weeping. Matt touched her on the shoulder and said, "Now, now!"

She threw her arms around him and clung tight to him, sobbing. "The brutes! The monsters! They're not human!"

He stroked her hair, soothing her until her hysteria had run its course. Presently she looked up at him, calming. "What can we do?" she asked plaintively.

She was still shaking, clinging to him. He lifted her in his arms and walked back toward the camp. Diamond and Shagrue, guns in their hands, had moved into the brush, but had halted and now turned and walked back toward the site of the camp when they saw him approaching, carrying the girl.

"I've thought of a stunt that might work," he whispered to her. "Then again it might not. It's all I can come up with. Running away won't do. You'll only be shot. You'll have to play along with me. Do you understand what I'm saying?"

"Of course," she murmured. "You can put me down now. I'm all right. I won't do anything like that again."

He continued to carry her. "This," he said, "is part of the scheme—the pleasant part."

Diamond said thinly to her when Matt carried

her into the camp, "You've run out your luck, girl. I told you the other day that another thing like this would be your last. I meant it."

Matt sat Nancy on her feet. "Let her alone," he said. "She wasn't trying to quit us. She was scared. After all, Diamond, how much do you think a woman can stand? This kind of a woman, at least. You should have stopped that fight."

Diamond eyed him intently. "I don't like the way you said that, my friend."

"Yeah? What didn't you like about it?"

"It sounded to me as though you might be getting some real soft ideas about this petticoat. Is that it?"

"That's it, I guess," Matt said.

Diamond didn't speak for a time. He had holstered his six-shooter. That had been a mistake, and he apparently was realizing it. He turned casually, presenting his left side to Matt. From that position he could draw and fire across his body while he offered the smallest possible target. A killer's maneuver.

"No!" Matt spoke. His own .45 was in his hand. It was cocked and pointed at Diamond's stomach.

"There's no need for you and me shooting at each other over this," Matt said. "Sure, I've fallen for this girl. But it's a two-way fall. She's going with me. All the way."

"What do you mean, all the way?" Diamond asked thinly.

"To South America," Matt said. He spoke to Nancy. "That's how it is, isn't it?"

She did not hesitate. "Yes," she said. "All the way." She turned to Diamond. "It happens that I wouldn't object in the least to having some of the better things of life, along with the rest of you. I've never had much easy living." She added, looking at Matt. "And I rather like him too."

She was convincingly bold. Even brassy. Shagrue stared and uttered a snicker. "Blast it, Battles!" he said, almost admiringly. "I knew dang well, all along, that there was somethin' goin' on betwixt you two."

Diamond pretended to be pleased also, but that was mainly because Matt, while he had lowered his six-shooter, continued to keep it in his hand.

Baldy, in the background, remained non-committal as usual, careful to avoid taking sides in a situation where the winner might be in doubt.

"Well, now," Diamond said. "This is very romantic. I give the both of you my blessing. But we've got to be practical. There are other matters to be taken care of. Exactly where do we go from here?"

Baldy spoke. "This here's about as fur as I can go, Doc. You've been promisin' me for days that I'd get my money when we got to this here Rainbow town. It seems like we're about there."

He added hastily, "Not that I ain't trustin' you, but I've got to git back to my place. Some o' the boys what helped us along the trail expect to git a little money from me on my way back."

Diamond eyed Matt. "How about it, Battles?"

Matt nodded. "All right. But it'll take a little more time. Maybe only a day. Maybe two. I can't say. I haven't got the money right under foot, you know."

Diamond nodded. "Baldy will wait. The important thing is to play it careful. Now that we've come this far, we don't intend to spoil it by making too fast a move. You understand that, don't you, Baldy?"

"Sure, sure," Baldy said gloomily. "I'll hang around for a while. Looks like I'll have to."

"I'll have to borrow your sorrel, Diamond," Matt said.

"What's the matter with that roan you've been riding?" Diamond demanded. "It's as good a horse as mine. Maybe better."

Matt looked at Nancy. She smiled and sidled closer to him, grasping his arm with both hands and pressing her cheek against his shoulder.

"The sorrel's for her," Matt said. "That bay she's been riding is too slow in case we hit trouble and have to make fast tracks."

Before Diamond could object, he added, "She's going with me."

"Do you think I'm a fool?" Diamond demanded. "We'd never see either of you again."

Matt shrugged. "That's a chance you have to

take." Baldy had retreated to a safe distance, believing that gunplay was in the making. He was out of earshot. Matt lowered his voice. "You know what will bring me back. That bullion you've got hid out up the line. You told it yourself. The bigger the stake we can throw together, the better our chances of making it to South America. Money talks. We might have to buy our way out of this country. We still want enough left to split up among us and have something worth while."

Money *was* talking. Diamond could appreciate this line of reasoning. It coincided with his own.

"But the girl stays here," he insisted. "She'll be safe enough. And it might help decide you to come back to us."

Matt looked at Shagrue, who had picked up a rifle. "I wouldn't trust either of you. She goes with me. She belongs to me. Get that straight now and for keeps. Take it or leave it."

He held the whiphand. They had to be rid of Baldy before they dared lift their bullion cache. He was their only hope of producing the money for which Baldy was waiting.

"Put down your gun, Shagrue," he said, "before I blow a hole in you. You can't kill me. That'd be like shooting the golden goose." He added, "Let's quit arguing, and get some sleep. I'll pull out right after dark. With luck, there's a chance I might be back, come daybreak."

"With the law on your trail, maybe," Diamond said.

"I'll guarantee I won't bring that down on you."

Diamond had to be satisfied with that. "Bring the girl back with you, and I'll believe you," he said. "If you're trying to run a high blaze on me, I'll make the both of you wish you'd never been born."

Shagrue and Baldy gave Ledge a lonely and unmarked burial in a dry wash by undermining a sandy cutbank and cascading a small avalanche down upon the shallow grave they had scratched.

"There's his slice o' the pie," Shagrue said with satisfaction. "Him an' his high an' mighty ways. He give me ten days in the snake pit once fer lookin' crosswise at him."

At dusk, Matt saddled the sorrel for Nancy and rigged his own horse. Diamond stood by in silence as they mounted.

"I'll be back," Matt said. "You can bank on that, Diamond."

They rode away into the darkness. Nancy drew a long, sighing breath when she was sure that no bullet was to follow them. "He almost believed you," she said.

"He can't do anything else but string along with us," Matt said. "He won't be convinced until I show up with a thousand dollars."

"You don't mean you actually intend to do that?"

"Of course."

"Are you saying you're going back there with the money?"

"What else? I've got to find out where they hid the bullion. Otherwise, I've got no real evidence they held up the train."

"And die trying to find this evidence."

He leaned from the saddle and peered close at her. "I'm going to do my damnedest to stay alive. And it would be a mighty sight tougher to go now than it would have been a while back."

"Since when?" she asked, her voice faint, shaky.

"You know the answer to that. Since it happened. But I'm beginning to see that it happened a lot longer ago than I figured. Maybe when we were kids, and I used to throw snowballs at you. You always seemed too far away, too good for a patched saddle ranch kid like me. A lady."

He drew her close to him. "You're still a lady," he said. "I told Diamond the truth about how I felt about you. All except the part about you going to South America with me."

"I'll go even there if you wish," she said.

"All I ask is that you wait for me in Rainbow." He added, "I mean, a reasonable length of time."

"But—?" she began. Then she kissed him. "I'll wait! A long time. A long, long time. Forever, if need be."

Presently she asked, "Where—how—can we get this money?"

"That's what I've been scratching my head about. I've got only one man in mind. Paul Wallford."

"Paul Wallford?" she echoed dubiously. "Why Paul?"

"That ought to be easy to see. He's more concerned than anyone else to find out who really killed his uncle."

"I suppose so," she said. "But if he's anything like he used to be, he'd like nothing better than to have you sent back to Stone Lodge."

Matt grinned in the darkness. "That's all over with. We didn't hit it off too well when we were kids, I'll admit. We had a few fist fights, but—"

"Over Mary Handley," she sniffed.

"All right, over Mary Handley. But we're grown up now. Paul's about the only one in Rainbow who would speak to me or act friendly since the train holdup."

"Likely he was hoping you'd confide in him so that he could turn you over to the law and get the reward," she said.

"Now, now," Matt said chidingly. "You're not being fair."

"All I know is that he was mean and selfish as a boy, and that he egged on that mob that tried to lynch you."

"After all, he had reason. It was his uncle that had been murdered."

"There must be someone else we can go to for money," she said. "Let me think. There's Charlie Bass, the wagon freighter. He's doing well, and he was a good friend of father's. I'm sure he would loan—"

"I'd say the chances of Charlie Bass having a thousand dollars in cash in his wallet are mighty thin. I want that money at once. Tonight. If we dally, Diamond might get spooky and do something I don't expect."

"But I feel that we should at least try."

"We can't just ride into town and tell people what we're there for. That would spoil everything. I've still got to string along with Diamond. It'll be around midnight before we get to town. That's a poor time to be asking for a loan. Paul is about our only hope. There's bound to be that much cash on hand in the safe at the store. I know where he lives. He likely isn't carrying that much money with him, but he can sneak down to the store and get it for us."

"If he'll do it," she said skeptically.

"There's still thirty thousand dollars missing," Matt said. "That's Paul's money and it ought to prod him into helping us. He inherited all of Cyrus Johnson's estate, but I understand that the biggest part of it turned out to be promissory notes and IOUs from ranchers and people that Cy loaned money to in order to keep them going. At least that's what I heard while I was waiting trial in Cedar Springs. Thirty thousand, if he could get it back, would put the store back on a sound basis again."

"But this wouldn't be getting it back," she said.

"No, but if he was convinced I didn't take the money, it would narrow down the field. Up to now, I've been the big he-wolf. They haven't thought of suspecting anyone else."

CHAPTER FOURTEEN

The lights of Rainbow were taking shape ahead. Their horses splashed across the clear waters of Butte Creek. They passed the clearing in which stood a square, brick schoolhouse which had a small bell tower. It was the school they had attended.

They rode onward in silence, a silence during which they were very close in thought, closer than Matt had ever been with any person. Between them was this capacity for understanding, for contentment in each other's company. For peace of mind.

"Who could have done it?" Nancy finally said, breaking the spell. "Who could have murdered Mr. Johnson?"

"I've asked myself that a thousand times," Matt said. "Ten thousand. It's still the first thing I think of in the morning, the last at night. I've tried to figure it out. All I get is nothing."

"Talk about it," she said. "Tell me about it. Not like you did in court. You were deliberately trying to appear guilty, to make sure they'd convict you. Tell me just how it all happened. Every detail."

Every detail! Matt let his thoughts drift back. Far back. It seemed so long ago. Yet, so vividly was it burned into his mind, every moment of it was sharp in his recollection.

"I was scared," he said. "More scared than I'd ever been in my life. More scared even than one day on the—"

He broke off. He hadn't meant to go into that. She took up the words. ". . . than one day on the Sweetwater River. The gunfight. I've heard about that."

"It's a thing I want to forget," he said. "But I never will. And I'll never forget that night in Rainbow. It was hot that evening, but I was shivering inside and cold. And icy sweat outside. After I had talked with your father I got my saddle and bedroll from the Eagle Hotel, then rustled a horse from Arch Caswell's *remuda*.

"I left the horse tied up back of the Great Western and walked into the street. I made sure nobody was near enough to worry about, and went into the store. The blinds in the big windows had been pulled down, but you could still see into the store through the glass in the doors.

"Cy Johnson was sitting at his desk in the office, with his back to me. The safe was open in the inner office. The safe looked like someone had turned it inside out. It wasn't until I was within reach of Cy Johnson that I realized something was wrong. I touched him, and his body began to slide from the chair. It was then that I saw the spike in his back."

He paused and said tiredly, "That's about all there was to it. At that moment somebody in the street spotted me and started yelling. I didn't know at the time that it was Paul Wallford. I ran for it. All I could think of was that they'd shoot me down. I guess I was lucky, for Paul testified at the trial that he wasn't armed. I got to my horse and cut the breeze out of town. I think you know the rest of it."

"I'm afraid I do," she said. "Father and I were eating supper in the Delmonico, keeping our fingers crossed, hoping nothing would go wrong. But it did. When we heard Paul yelling, Father rushed out. By the time he found out that Mr. Johnson had been murdered, you had gotten away."

"Clearing out in a hurry was about the only thing I did right," Matt sighed. "I'd never make a holdup man. A real one. I tripped over my spur a couple of times as I was stampeding out of there. I spooked my horse so that he almost piled me when I got aboard. I didn't know until later that my mask had slipped off my face during the excitement. I didn't even know I had been burned."

"Burned?"

"A live cigar that Cy Johnson had been smoking was in an ash tray beside him. I must have put the heel of my hand on its business end when I grabbed him to keep him from falling out of the chair. But I didn't know until later what I'd done. I had a blister as big as a half dollar for a couple of days."

The first outlying habitations of Rainbow were looming ahead. A dog began barking. Matt veered the horses away from that vicinity. The dog quieted.

"Somebody drove that spike into Cy Johnson's back not many minutes before I went into the store," he said. "Cy couldn't have been dead long."

"The fact that a miner's candlestick was used seems to show that it hadn't been planned beforehand," she said. "At least it looks that way. Somebody saw his chance all of a sudden, picked up the nearest weapon and used it. Maybe that person was still in the store when you came in and sneaked away while you were inside the office. Did you see anything? Hear anything?"

"An elephant might have been in the place without me seeing it," Matt said. "I just got through telling you that I was plenty steamed up and as clumsy as a hog on slick ice."

"What if Paul Wallford doesn't believe you?"

"How can he doubt *you*?" Matt demanded.

"Paul isn't the sort to go out of his way to be fair if he thinks he's got an advantage. You, above all, should know that."

"I tell you he's grown up now. He wouldn't let schoolboy grudges prod him into trying to keep a murder charge hanging over me if he knew I was innocent."

Nancy was silent. He knew she was still dubious. The truth was that the same doubt racked him. Even with Nancy to corroborate his story that her father had arranged the fake holdup, the real issue might not change. Paul Wallford—and the world—might still believe that the sight of so much money had been too great an allure for him.

"Mr. Johnson was a fine man," she said. "So many men gave testimony to that at his funeral service. He was a Mormon elder, you know, in the church here at Rainbow. The Mormons always pay personal tribute to their dead at the funeral. I only hope my father's burial was as impressive, even though he wasn't of the Mormon belief."

She suddenly choked up. Matt placed a hand on her arm. He knew that she was thinking that she did not even know where or when her father had been buried.

"We better leave the horses here," he said gently. He dismounted and lifted her from the saddle. He tethered the horses in the shelter of brush on the fringe of town.

Nancy suddenly clutched his arm excitedly. "That cigar! The one in the ash tray that burned your hand. It couldn't have been Mr. Johnson's!"

"Why not?"

"Because it's against his religion to smoke. You say it was still burning? And on his desk?"

Matt stiffened. "Of course!" he breathed. "Why, of course!"

"Whoever left it there must have been a person very close to Mr. Johnson," she said, her voice shaking. "Someone he trusted. They must have been talking at his desk, just before the murder." She added in a whisper, "That person killed Mr. Johnson."

Matt stood remembering. "It was good tobacco," he said. "Rich. Fragrant. I recall that much." But there was something else about that cigar that now eluded him. Some peculiarity.

"Paul Wallford smokes cigars," Nancy said. "I've seen him smoking them. He isn't a Mormon."

Matt stared at her. "It just can't be."

"But it is," she breathed. "When he testified that he'd just come back to the store and saw you inside, he lied. He had been there earlier. His uncle probably had to tell him that a fake holdup was to be staged, for fear he would interfere. He saw his chance to do away with his uncle and inherit the store. And also to get away with thirty thousand dollars in cash, just in case he might be disappointed when his uncle's will was read, or about the size of the estate."

"We can't accuse a man on flimsy evidence."

"I know I'm right," she said impatiently.

He nodded agreement. "That's why he knew I was hiding out in the sheriff's room at the Mountain House that morning after the murder. He figured I'd try to get in touch with your father, and likely kept track of him and saw me sneak into the hotel before daybreak. He waited until he thought your father had ridden out of town, then tried to get me lynched. He's the one who tried to pick us off from the loft of the Great Western feed barn. He could get in and out of the barn through the store from the Gulch side without anybody being the wiser."

"But we've still got no legal proof," she said drearily. "What can we do?"

"The same as before," Matt said. "Talk Paul into rounding up the thousand dollars. Or force him. Play along with Diamond until I find out where they hid the bullion. That means more to the people around Rainbow than anything else."

They moved through side lanes, with every shadow looming black and menacing, with every distant footfall driving them to cover until the threat had passed.

Matt knew that Paul Wallford had occupied a bachelor's cottage on First Chance Gulch beyond the east fringe of the business area. But, when they reached it, they found the place dark and unoccupied.

"He's moved away," Nancy sobbed. "But where?"

"I've got an idea," Matt said.

The more pretentious home that Cyrus Johnson had occupied was a short distance farther east. They made their way there. It was a pretentious, two-story house with a veranda. It sat well back from the sidewalk among oaks and box elders and surrounded by a picket fence. A driveway led to a carriage house and stable at the rear.

The name PAUL WALLFORD was painted on the wooden arch over the iron gate that opened onto the brick walk leading to the steps of the veranda.

"He's not only wearing his uncle's boots, but he's moved into his uncle's house," Matt commented.

A lamp burned in the entry area of the house, but there was no other light. Matt unlatched the gate and tiptoed up the brick walk and onto the veranda. He stood for a space, listening, but there was no sound in the house. He twisted the brass key of the door bell. The metallic sound rang emptily in the rooms. But there was no response.

Nancy waited in the shadows while he scouted the yard. "Paul must be in town," he reported to her on his return. "His pacer and buggy are in the stable. Likely he's playing poker."

"Or calling on Mary Handley," Nancy said.

Matt peered at her. "Who's Mary Handley?"

Despite her weariness, Nancy giggled. "You have a short memory. Are we going to wait here?"

"Yes. At least until I can figure out something else to do. He may show up."

They found a bench in darkness alongside the house. Nancy fell asleep almost at once, her head on his shoulder.

Their wait was not long. Matt awakened her, his finger on her lips to silence her. Someone on foot was approaching on the sidewalk. Brisk footsteps turned in at the gate and moved up the walk to the porch. A key ring jangled. Paul Wallford had returned.

Matt moved fast. He reached the veranda steps and mounted as Wallford opened the door.

"Hello Paul!" he said.

Wallford whirled. He was outlined against the light of the lamp in the hall, but Matt was still in shadow.

"It's Matt Battles," Matt said.

Paul Wallford stood frozen for an instant, then made a frenzied motion toward the breast of his coat. He was trying to draw a gun. The lamplight fell full on his face and Matt saw something he had never seen before in a human expression—total fear—complete desperation.

He seized Wallford's arm, preventing him from drawing the weapon that he had in a shoulder holster. "I've got a gun too, Paul," he said. "But I didn't come here to do any shooting." He reached inside the man's coat and removed the weapon from an armpit holster. "Just to make sure we can talk friendly," he added. "Take it easy, Paul. I didn't come here to start trouble."

Nancy joined Matt. Wallford gazed at her and now there was horror in him that was almost terrifying. And despair.

"We're not ghosts, Paul," Matt said.

Wallford wore a Panama hat, a tailored suit, and expensive linen. He had a diamond stickpin in his tie. He had been smoking a cigar, but had dropped it when Matt's appearance had startled him.

Matt lifted a foot to crush out the glowing tip of the cigar which lay on the waxed maple floor of the hallway. Then he bent, peering closer at the band on the cigar. It was of silvered material, formed in the shape of a chain with the small label bearing the insignia and the name of its Havana manufacturer.

He straightened. He was now recalling the detail that had eluded him when he was recounting the events of Cyrus Johnson's death.

"I see you still smoke these good Havanas, Paul," he said. "I guess you order them special, don't you?"

Wallford was gazing at Nancy too stunned to comprehend what Matt had said. "My God!" he mumbled hollowly. "I thought—"

"That we were dead," Nancy said. "But we're very much alive, Paul."

254

Matt pushed the ashen-faced man farther into the hall and on into the elaborately furnished parlor. He said to Nancy, "Close the door and draw the curtains."

Wallford tried to pull himself together. "You've been given up for dead, Nancy," he said. "We heard you'd been kidnaped by this fellow and other convicts when they broke out of prison. What's this all about?"

"It's too long a story to tell right now," Matt said. "We came here for something else. I need a thousand dollars."

"A thousand dollars?"

"Just a loan, Paul. I'll pay it back."

Wallford could only stare blankly. "You've got it," Matt said. "I need it. Tonight. At once."

Wallford spoke numbly, "What did you say?"

Matt shook him. "Listen to me! I want a thousand dollars. In cash."

Wallford's mind began working. "I don't understand," he said. "What do you need a—?"

"Never mind that," Matt snapped. "I can't waste time explaining."

"Where would I get that much money at this time of night?"

He saw the expression on Matt's face and hastily added, "I might be able to rake up a hundred dollars or so here in the house. But a thousand . . ."

He was lying. Matt looked at Nancy. He saw in

255

her eyes the same thought that was in him. They were both suddenly sure, beyond all doubt, that it had been Wallford who had murdered his uncle that night and looted the safe. It was written on him. Guilt. Fear of punishment.

Matt moved into the hallway, picked up the still-burning cigar and tossed it into an ash tray on the table which held the ashes and stubs of other smokes. "You're mighty careless about leaving live cigars lying around, Paul," he said.

He saw the flicker of new despair in Wallford. The man knew what he meant. Wallford *did* remember that cigar. It had been his one mistake.

"I've been thinking over what happened the night your uncle was murdered, Paul," Matt said. "Exactly where were you at the time?"

"What are you trying to do?" Wallford demanded. "I wasn't within blocks of the store. I was at my place, shaving."

"Could you prove that, Paul, if the sheriff began asking you to do so?"

"If you're trying to hang anything on me, Matt, you're insane. Why, you admitted the whole thing in court."

"Not exactly," Matt said. "I admitted nothing. I just didn't deny it."

"Then what are you driving at?"

"All I'm asking, Paul, is the loan of a thousand dollars."

Wallford hesitated. That was enough. Matt

was now not only sure he was guilty, but that the money was near at hand. Concealed in, or close to, this house, probably.

Cyrus Johnson's own home would be about the last place that would be suspected as the hiding place of the money that had vanished at the time of his murder. Wallford had known that he must let the passage of time end all chance of arousing suspicion before attempting to make use of that source of riches.

"Fetch the thousand, Paul," Matt said. "I know you have it. Fetch it, or we'll tear this place to pieces to find it."

"I tell you I haven't got it!" Wallford protested.

Matt nodded to Nancy. "Begin hunting."

She walked to a highboy, pulled out a drawer and emptied the contents on the floor. The drawer contained only tintypes and other relics that evidently had been the keepsakes of Cyrus Johnson. She emptied a second drawer with the same result.

"Hold on!" Wallford exclaimed. "What's the matter with you, Nancy? You're as crazy as Battles. I don't want my house wrecked."

"That's up to you," Matt said. "Keep searching, Nancy."

"All right," Wallford said sullenly. "I *do* have a little extra cash hid out. Maybe not as much as a thousand. I'll take a look."

"Where?"

Wallford hesitated. "Upstairs," he finally said. "I'll fetch down what I can find."

He headed for the stairs which led from the hall to the upper rooms. He halted when he saw that Matt was following him.

"There's no need for you to go up," he said.

"I'm going," Matt answered.

"I can't get away, if that's what's worrying you. There's no other way down, except by these stairs. And I'm not going to break a leg by jumping out of a window."

Again Matt nodded to Nancy. "Take a look!"

Lighting a table lamp and carrying it, she inspected the entire lower floor. "There's no back stairs," she reported. "I guess he's telling the truth—for once."

Matt was sure he knew why Wallford insisted that he be allowed to get the money unobserved. This was not the time to press their luck, however.

"All right," he said. "I'll stay down here. But make it fast."

He and Nancy waited at the foot of the stairs. Wallford went above and lighted a lamp which he carried down an upper hall. The dance of the shadows faded and they heard a door open. Then came the creak of more steps.

"It's hid in the attic," Matt murmured. "The filthy murderer. His own uncle. And living in his uncle's house with the blood money, waiting until it was safe to spend it."

They could faintly hear objects being moved in the attic. A short period of silence followed.

Then the steps creaked again, the lamp shadows danced once more. Wallford appeared. There were smudges of dust and streaks of cobwebs on his Panama and linen.

He descended the stairs and petulantly thrust into Matt's hand a roll of bills. "There it is," he said. "It's every last cent I could find in the house. Lucky for you, I had a winning streak in a poker game only last night."

Matt counted the money. There were ten fifty-dollar bills, with the remainder in twenties and tens. "You play in a fast game, Paul," he commented, thumbing the fifty-dollar greenbacks. "You *do* need luck, gambling for that kind of money."

"You're forcing me to give this to you, with a gun in your hand, Battles," Wallford said. "Remember that."

"I told you it was only a loan," Matt said.

"The law won't look at it that way."

"Now, Paul," Matt said. "If you went to law about this, it might mean that the law might start nosing around in the attic up there. No telling what might be found."

He stuffed the roll of bills inside his shirt. "You ought to learn to trust more in banks, Paul," he added. "But you never were one to trust anybody."

He and Nancy moved toward the door. "Don't try to follow us, Paul," Matt said. "Don't come out of that door for ten minutes, at least. Count up to about, let's say thirty thousand dollars before you make any kind of a move."

He and Nancy left by the front door. They hurried down the walk and let themselves out by way of the iron gate then headed west along the clay sidewalk.

Once they were hidden from the house by trees and a hedge, Matt halted. "I've got a hunch our friend isn't going to do any counting before he makes his next move," he murmured. "Let's linger a while. I think he'll be running scared—trying to find a new hiding place for that money."

There were other houses in the vicinity, all dark, their inmates asleep. He and Nancy crouched in the shadow of the hedge that adjoined the driveway of Paul Wallford's house, waiting.

Matt's fingers tightened on Nancy's arm. Wallford hadn't wasted time going into action. They could hear faint sounds from the stable. A horse was being harnessed to a carriage. Wallford evidently had rushed directly to the stable by way of a rear door. But no light showed. He was working in darkness, and evidently was taking some pains to be quiet.

A lull came. Then they were sure they saw a light moving in the house and in the attic. That vanished, too, and they heard Wallford return to the stable. The hinges of the wide carriage door creaked as the portal was opened.

The street gate of the driveway had not been closed for the night. The rig emerged abruptly from the stable at the rear, came down the driveway with wheels crunching gravel. A whip was used and the horse broke into a frightened gallop.

Paul Wallford was in the buggy, and he was cursing in a low, savage tone as he used the whip again. The vehicle careened into the unpaved street, the spirited horse demoralized by the wildness of the driver and the unexpected punishment.

Wallford yanked the animal around, intending to head out of town. The buggy, its wheels cut short, tilted, but settled back.

Matt leaped from the shadows and completed the horse's panic. He caught the animal's bit, jerking its head around. It reared, terrified, recoiling from him.

That again cramped the wheels of the buggy and this time the vehicle capsized. Wallford tried to leap clear but landed heavily on his head and shoulders in the dust. He lay gasping.

The horse, bucking wildly, broke the shafts and stampeded down the street into the darkness. Wallford still sprawled, wheezing for the breath that had been jolted out of him.

A white pillowcase had been thrown from

the buggy also and it lay beside Wallford in the street. It was well-stuffed.

Matt picked up the pillowcase and emptied its contents into the light night breeze. It had been filled with banknotes. The money sailed like leaves, scattering over Wallford and over the street.

Matt drew his six-shooter and fired two shots into the air. The reports were deafening in the night silence. He caught Nancy's arm and they fled off the street and between houses into the back lanes. He could hear sleepers in the houses awakening and calling out.

"What's goin' on out there?" a man shouted. Doors were opening and they could hear voices in the street.

Nancy began to laugh hysterically. "Now they'll know!" she gasped as they ran. "He's lying in his bed of blood money. Let him explain that to his neighbors."

Matt slowed the pace. Back of them they could hear more voices. Voices that were growing excited. And asking questions.

These sounds faded behind them. They made their way to the fringe of town and found their horses standing hipshot and drowsy and undisturbed where they had left them.

Matt drew Nancy into his arms and kissed her. "This might take a little time," he said. "Maybe a week or so. I don't know. I've no way of knowing. Stay here in Rainbow until I come back."

"*If* you come back," she said drearily. "Diamond. Shagrue. They won't be taken alive. Not by you. They're two to one. What's the need of dying?"

"You know the answer to that. And I don't aim to die. You know that, too. And you know why."

"I know the answer," she said. "Johnny Kidd."

"I've got to know where he is. I've got to find him. I owe him that much. Johnny's already given me years of life that I wouldn't have, but for what he did."

"He gave you a hundred years in dungeons on the Hill," she said bitterly. "How long do you have to keep paying him back for saving your life?"

"He'd do the same for me," Matt said.

"So you've told me before. And I say to let cold trails stay cold. All you'll find is heartbreak when you find him. They'll hang him for being in on the robbery."

"Johnny's dead," Matt said. "I feel that. I know it."

"But the—"

"The post card? I admit I can't explain that. I'll never rest easy until I know. Johnny just couldn't have been in on the holdup with them. He wasn't that kind. And then there's the bullion. Think what it will do for people around here if I can bring it back."

"I'm going—" she began. But whatever she had in mind, she decided not to continue with it.

She clung to him for a time. Her tears were warm on his cheek.

"I'll be back," he told her. He kept repeating it. But in him was the desolate thought that this was their final parting and that they would never again be in each other's arms.

"I'll come back—somehow," he said.

"Of course," she said. "Oh, of course." She finally released him. And then burst into sobbing that she could not control.

He lifted her onto the sorrel, and mounted his roan. She was still sitting there in the shadows of the brush, with the scattered lights of Rainbow in the background when he looked back.

CHAPTER FIFTEEN

He rode toward the camp in the brush where Diamond and Shagrue and Baldy would be waiting. The lights of Rainbow receded into the well of blackness, appearing, reappearing as he crested the swells in the land until he could see them no more, leaving the range, the mighty range, bleak and lonely beneath the sable sky.

He looked at the glittering stars and remembered the great days of the past. Of snowballing a spindle-legged, pigtailed little spitfire on the way to and from the schoolhouse on Butte Creek and of fleeing from her wrath. Of riding far out of his way on the wild colt that was his personal mount as a boy, in order to escort Mary Handley to the schoolhouse. And how he had envied Paul Wallford, who had usually stood higher in Mary's favor.

He remembered Johnny Kidd and their escapades. And the spice of the range war when he and Johnny had learned what the face of danger looked like, a vision that changed a man and set him apart from the ordinary run of humanity.

Gun swift! That was the reputation he had earned along with Johnny. He recalled that day of smoking weapons and death. Life had been sweet at that moment, but not as sweet as now. For there had been no Nancy Chisholm waiting for him then.

He remembered the year of ostracism after the train holdup. He remembered Stone Lodge. And Ed Ledge, who lay in a shallow grave on the backtrail. And Frank Welton in his clammy tomb. And Tex Texas. Who had Tex Texas really been? It did not matter now. He was gone from the face of the earth. Likely no one cared. He had stepped briefly into Doc Diamond's path and had been brushed aside, erased forever.

Eagle Peak's summit took on a cold, silvery tinge. It was always the first to gather to itself the promise of the new day, the first to announce that the night was over.

The tops of the Rainbows caught the light and swam in the lingering mists of the night like a fleet of galleons. The mists faded and all of the land, gray-green, windless, and motionless lay silently before him. He was the only speck that moved beneath the great sky which was now turning the color of polished steel.

Ahead loomed the green hue of the brush that grew along the creek where Diamond probably already had spotted him. He made out the faint stain of smoke from a cookfire that was being doused with water, now that daybreak might reveal its presence.

They were still there. Waiting. Waiting beneath

the vast, free sky which was now pale blue in hue.

Something caused him to twist in the saddle. A presentiment of being watched. A rider had appeared far away over a rise, behind him but off his direct backtrail. A rider who was astride, but wore skirts. Nancy! He was no longer alone.

She had trailed him, keeping out of sight until she was sure it was too late to be sent back. He waited until she rode up to join him. Her eyes were underscored by dark circles. Weariness had thinned her face so that all that was left alive were the fires of affection and determination.

"This is the way love is," she said. "I never knew before how it would be. Now, I'm happy again."

There was no reproach in him. He only wished she had not loved this much. For, if she were to die, there would be no real life for him, even if he happened to live.

She saw this knowledge in him. She smiled and touched his face with her fingers. "There must be no sadness, no self-reproach, no matter what happens," she said. "For either of us. If only one of us goes back, there is to be no mourning. Only memories of what we meant to each other."

He said, "Yes." Then they rode ahead toward the brush. As they neared the willows, Diamond stepped into view. Shagrue appeared beyond him, partly shielded by a boulder. Shagrue had a rifle in his hands.

Diamond packed a brace of six-shooters. He had carried only a single side gun during the long journey, but had now armed himself with the .45 that had belonged to Ledge.

The guns bulked on his thighs, mechanically sinister in the dawn light where there were no shadows, no color.

Matt spoke, "A cold reception committee."

Diamond gazed at Nancy and wagged his head in wonder. "I bet Turk a thousand dollars of my share that the girl would never come back with you," he said. "I thought she was lying."

"You're a poor judge of people," Matt said. He drew from his shirt the roll of bills and tossed it to Diamond. "You lose your bet, but speaking of a thousand," he added, "here's Baldy's money."

The ugliness faded out of Diamond. He slapped Matt on the back. He counted the money into Baldy's hands and said, "Now slope out of here. You've got your fee. Don't try to follow us."

"Only an idjit would follow a trail as hot as yours," Baldy snorted. He hastened to saddle up and rode away without another word, gigging his horse with a spur. He never looked back.

"Where did you get the *dinero*?" Diamond asked.

"I got it," Matt said tersely.

Diamond smiled. "And there's more where it came from. About twenty-nine thousand dollars, I'd say."

"Right now all I say is that Nancy and myself need some grub and some rest."

"And I say that I hope you've hid the twenty-nine thousand somewhere close so that it can be picked up easy when the time comes," Diamond said. "As I understand our agreement, it goes toward sweetening the pot."

"You'll see it when the time comes," Matt said.

"We're going to need it," Diamond said. "Ready cash will be mighty handy. You can't just walk into a store and use bullion to buy what we need. It'll take a little time to get our money out of the bars."

"I saw the smoke of your fire as I was riding in," Matt said. "None of us might ever see the money or the bullion if you keep on being careless. Letting smoke show at daybreak is a good way of putting your head in a noose. But, if there's any coffee still warm, we'd say maybe it was worth the risk. Even those cold flapjacks look good."

"Of course," Diamond said. "A man forgets his manners, leading this kind of a life. Eat, drink, and be merry."

Nancy spoke. "For tomorrow we die?"

"Now, now, my dear!" Diamond said chidingly. "No morbid thoughts. I'm happy that you're

269

going with us. South America seems much more attractive to me. To all of us."

He patted her shoulder. Nancy pushed his hand away. "I suppose they even have pests in South America," she said. "The human variety, I mean."

Diamond laughed. "And generous people," he said.

He was not finished with Nancy. He was no longer looking on her as a handicap, now that she was no longer needed as a shield. He was looking at her as a desirable woman.

Matt gazed stonily. Diamond glanced at him. Their eyes met. Both of them admitted silently the truth they did not want to bring into the open. Between them was no bond except the bullion and Matt's supposed cache of greenbacks. Beyond that was death for one or the other. Perhaps both.

Nancy saw this, too. The dread that was always in her came to the surface. The dark cloud touched even Shagrue's slow mind. He peered, blinking. He was sobered by the realization that he might be called on to choose sides in a duel where the winner took all.

They remained in the hideout during the day. When dusk came they saddled and pulled out. They circled Rainbow, avoiding ranchhouses and crossing trails only after making sure they were leaving no trace of their passage.

Nancy remained close at Matt's side. They

were traveling through familiar country, a country where they had their roots. The black outlines of the ridges against the stars formed patterns they had known as children. The roads they crossed, whose dry dust was white against the black background of timber, were roads they had ridden in the carefree days of the past.

They camped again at dawn and traveled once more during a long, black, cloudy night. A driving rain, cold and drenching, beat at them after midnight. Toward morning they reached the main line of the Dakota Pacific east of Cedar Springs.

They camped for another day, wrapped in damp blankets under slickers, and traveled eastward at night, paralleling the railroad. The rain ended and the sky cleared. Diamond and Shagrue were halting their tired horses often now, peering at the ridges and consulting each other about landmarks. The end of the long trail was near.

Finally Diamond said, "We'll hang up until it's light enough to see. We're not sure just where we are."

They drew the rigs from their mounts. Matt and Nancy used their saddles as pillows, and pretended to doze in their blankets, but they were tensely awake and alert.

Diamond and Shagrue were sleepless, driven by a high excitement that loosened their tongues. The thought of the wealth that was so near intoxicated them. They had escaped from prison, outwitted pursuit and were near their goal. They were seeing their dreams of a life of ease fulfilled. They needed no alcohol, so high were their spirits.

Diamond shed his steel shell. Once again he became a boastful ruffian who tried to impress Matt, and especially Nancy, with his stories of mighty feats as an outlaw and a gunman. This time his mood was genuine. It was real, vainglorious Diamond who was talking.

"You're in fast company, Battles," he told Matt. "I've taken care of five men who thought they were fast. I've stuck up stages. But the best haul I ever made was right here on this stretch of railroad track. Remember that water tank we passed a few miles back? That's where we showed up on the engine of a Dakota Pacific express and got ourselves a pile of gold bigger than you could lift."

He looked at Nancy. "We'll have money enough to carpet a room when we cash in that bullion," he went on. "Maybe I'll do just that, someday. I'll let you walk on it in your pretty bare feet."

"It's about time," Nancy said. "We've come a long way. Just where is this carpet of money?"

"Mighty close," Diamond said. "Mighty, mighty close. It'll be easy to find as soon as it gets light."

"How did you swing the thing?" Matt asked. "I know that you had to do some shooting."

"The engineer got smart and tried to jam on the whistle, so as to blow steam and stop us from moving the express car down the line away from the rest of the train," Diamond said.

"I settled his beer fer him," Shagrue said. "He was a blasted fool. I knew him personal. Used to railroad with him. I was a brakeman on the D.P. Knew the fireman too. An' he knew me. He made the mistake o' tellin' me so. You just can't leave people like that around."

Matt knew that Nancy was breathing a trifle fast. For the first time they were hearing the story of the train holdup. Matt took a chance, opening up a subject that he had carefully avoided in the past, fearing it might arouse Diamond's suspicion. But the moment seemed right.

"The shotgun messenger was in on it with you, as I recall it," he said. "I suppose he took his cut of the gold and is already in South America."

Both Diamond and Shagrue laughed. "We read in the newspapers that it was supposed to have been an inside job," Diamond said. "It wasn't. Not by a long shot. I figured out the whole thing. Me, Doc Diamond. I didn't need help from any sixty-dollar-a-month shotgun guard."

Shagrue slapped his thigh. "The john laws swallered that bait right up to the sinker," he chortled. He hesitated and added, "There ain't any reason for not tellin' about it now, is there, Doc? I mean about the post card?"

"Go ahead," Diamond said. "Tell it! You've been busting to brag about it for a long time."

"Battles, you bein' from Rainbow, you likely must know a jigger around there that they call Bucko?" Shagrue asked.

Matt had to fight to remain casual. "Bucko?" he repeated. "Why, yes. There was a cowboy I knew who answered to that handle. Rode for the Box Q. The boys called him Bucko because he was pretty good at handling bad horses."

"We sent this Bucko a post card once," Shagrue said.

Matt was wire taut. "Post card? Then you know him?"

"Never laid eyes on the fella, but we shore sent him somethin' to remember us by. It was Doc's idea. He figured the law would find out about that post card an' would waste time an' horses tryin' to find this here John Kidd."

"John Kidd?" Matt echoed. "Seems to me that was the name of the shotgun guard who was in cahoots with you two in the stickup."

Diamond spoke impatiently. "I tell you nobody was in on it with us. We used the post card to set up a blind trail. And it worked. We got away, clean."

"I don't savvy," Matt said.

"We didn't even know the name of the shotgun man until we read it in the newspapers. I'll say one thing for this John Kidd. He was a game little rooster for a cripple. Foolish, but game. He didn't have a chance. He was sitting at a little desk in the express car, writing this post card when we stepped in. It was addressed to this Bucko party at Rainbow. I guess Bucko must have been a pal of his, and the post card was aimed at joshing him, for it showed a buckaroo being piled into a bunch of cactus by a bronk. John Kidd intended to mail it somewhere along the way, I suppose."

"When you *stepped* in?" Matt asked. "You mean it was *that* easy to get into the express car?"

"That was why they thought the gun guard let us in," Diamond said, smiling. "Any car would have been easy to get into if it had got the treatment I gave it. They kept it on a siding at Cedar Springs between runs, empty and usually unlocked. It was an old rattletrap in the first place. It had doors set in each end that weren't used, but were kept bolted from the inside. I spent a lot of time there at nights, loosening the rusty screws and bolts that held the locks and hinges. I covered up the work with soap that I colored with rust."

"Smart," Matt said. "Very smart."

"It was a pushover. We waited until we were sure there would be money aboard. The only time they carried a shotgun guard was when there was treasure in the safe. We boarded the train as it was leaving Cedar Springs. Frank Welton and myself rode blind baggage next to the express car. Turk took care of the engine. The door on the express car popped open when I touched it with a pry bar."

He shrugged. "This John Kidd had set his shotgun in a rack across the car while he was writing this post card. He didn't have a chance. But he was fool enough to try for it."

He added, "After all, it wasn't his treasure he was trying to protect."

Matt was silent for a time. "What about the post card?" he asked.

"We took it with us and mailed it in Cheyenne about two weeks later. I figured that it would be shown to the sheriff up in these parts and that he'd run down a lot of blind trails trying to find that shotgun guard."

"There were a lot of rumors around Rainbow that this Bucko was in on the job, too," Matt said.

"Did you hear that, Doc?" Shagrue said, beaming. "They was lookin' for everybody but us."

"But what about the gun guard?" Matt asked. "This John Kidd. I knew him by sight. It was common talk around Rainbow that he was still alive. Word of that post card must have leaked out."

Diamond shrugged. "It was raining hard that night," he said. "A gully washer. That's one reason they were never able to find our tracks.

The rain covered all trails. We unhooked the express car, ran it ahead a dozen miles or so to where the railroad crosses the Big Sandy River. There we could blow the safe in peace. I'm afraid we gave the fellow a pretty damp grave. It seems like they never found a trace of him. The Big Sandy was wild and high that night."

Diamond was silent for a space. "That reminds me of Frank Welton," he said musingly. "I wonder if they ever found poor Frank's body."

He quit talking. Matt sat with his arms wrapped around his knees. Nancy lay quiet, but her hand went out, touching his arm, counseling caution. That helped. The thirst to take vengeance for Johnny's murder was a dark fire within him.

So that was how Johnny the Kid had died. Shot down while trying to get to his gun. His body tossed into a flooded river at night.

Matt fought back the rage and forced himself to wait.

Dawn was in the sky. Diamond aroused and gazed around. "It won't be long now," he said.

Daylight strengthened. In the distance a train whistle moaned. A dirge for Johnny Kidd.

Diamond and Shagrue were on their feet, moving with feverish restlessness. They peered impatiently, picking out landmarks as they emerged from the mists of the night. Peaks and ridges. And trees.

"We hit it right on the nose!" Diamond exclaimed triumphantly. "It's right over there in that stand of rocks!"

He began running, with Shagrue at his heels. Matt looked at Nancy. She came to him and kissed him with cold, ashen lips. But she did not try to halt him. She did not even speak. She followed slowly, at a distance, as he hurried in the wake of the running men. Diamond and Shagrue made their way to the base of one of the massive outcrops of weathered boulders that were a feature of this region. This particular landmark rose perhaps fifty feet at its crest and stood alone above an expanse of sagebrush.

Diamond halted, peering around. He and Shagrue began excitedly taking bearings. Matt stood a short distance away, waiting. The locomotive whistle wailed mournfully again. He could hear the muted drone of a train as it toiled across the plains far in the distance.

Diamond began pacing off steps. "Twenty-eight, twenty-nine, thirty!" he said.

The point he had reached was beneath the overhang of big slabs of rock that formed an alcove out of reach of the weather.

"Right where it should be," Diamond said. "Look for the shovel, Turk! It's hidden somewhere above us among the rocks."

Shagrue climbed the stand of boulders, grunting with the exertion and perspiring with excitement.

He peered into crevices, with Diamond calling instructions.

Finally, Shagrue shouted, "All right! It's still here!"

He vanished for a moment, then appeared, gripping a miner's shovel. The implement was rusty, its handle weathered after a year's time, but it was still serviceable.

"Dig right here, Turk!" Diamond said, his voice hoarse with excitement.

The spot he indicated was at the rear of the alcove where the overhang was so low that Shagrue had to work almost on his knees until he had formed an excavation large enough in which to stand upright. The soil was loose and dry.

Shagrue worked frenziedly, cursing when loose soil slid back into the opening, adding to his task.

Then they all heard it. The solid sound of the shovel striking metal. Shagrue looked up at Diamond. "It's still here!" he croaked joyfully.

He dug again with frantic speed. Presently, he muscled a corroded metal express box into view. Its lock had been broken before it had been cached.

He hurled the lid back. Matt saw that the box was filled with bullion bars.

Shagrue began laughing wildly. "Purty, ain't it?" he babbled. "Purtier'n a gal in a silk dress. Purtier'n—"

He looked up at Diamond and froze. He had

laid his rifle and .45 aside while he had been wielding the shovel. They were out of reach.

Diamond had moved back a pace or two. His right hand was hanging near a holster. In him was the implacable purpose that brought to Matt the memory of those moments when Frank Welton and Tex Texas had died. And now Shagrue was discovering that he had perhaps dug his own grave.

Matt spoke. "Don't do it, Diamond. Don't try it!" Diamond's gaze, dark, fierce, centered on him. Diamond studied him, trying to read the situation, appraising it carefully to see if there was any disadvantage for himself that he might have overlooked.

He decided there was none. Matt had made no move toward his holster.

Matt spoke to Shagrue without taking his eyes away from Diamond. "You know him a little better now, Turk. He was going to kill you. He never intended to split the stuff up with you."

Shagrue tried to climb out of the thigh-deep excavation in stumbling haste, but the sandy rim gave way and he floundered back.

"Stay there, Turk," Diamond advised him. "It'll save me some trouble."

"My God, Doc!" Shagrue chattered. "We're pals! You ain't goin' to kill me, are you? Why?"

"He's not going to kill you," Matt said. "But I

will if you make a wrong move. Stay where you are until I tell you what to do."

Nancy was well to Matt's right. She started to move nearer, intending to take possession of Shagrue's guns. "No!" Matt said. "Keep back!"

She halted, standing frozen, but out of the line of fire.

Diamond spoke. "I always knew you were ambitious, Battles. You're after the whole pot, aren't you? Your money and the bullion. I should have killed you days ago. I had many chances. That was a mistake."

"You made a lot of mistakes," Matt said. "Such as sending post cards."

Diamond stiffened. A dark doubt seemed to cross his mind. Doubt of himself, of his superiority over his opponent. "Post card?" he repeated, his brows lifting.

"I'm Bucko," Matt said.

For a space nobody spoke. Shagrue, in his sandy excavation, drew a grunting sigh, his slow mind beginning to grasp what this meant.

Diamond had known instantly what it meant. His eyes darted to Nancy, then back. "I'm beginning to see it," he said. "Do you know, Battles, I felt it inside me, right from the start. You never quite rang true. But I wouldn't believe my own good sense."

"That thirty-thousand-dollar bait was too much for you," Matt said.

281

"So that was a blind too," Diamond said wryly. "You were planted on the Hill. By that new warden. Somehow they'd found out I was the one who'd pulled that train stickup. You went into the Lodge to bait me into leading you here."

"Johnny Kidd was a friend of mine," Matt said. "Do you remember his face? The scars? And his hand. Crippled. He got all that saving my life in a range fire."

He added, "Don't go for your gun, Diamond. You'll lose. I'm younger, faster."

"There never was any thirty thousand in this fake cache of yours, was there?" Diamond said. "You played me for a fool right from the start."

"Now that was the odd part of it," Matt said. "There *was* thirty thousand in it. I never saw it myself until the other night in Rainbow. And you'll *never* see it, Diamond. We'll also get back the thousand we handed to Baldy and give him a taste of Stone Lodge. As for the rest of the money, it was scattered all over a street in Rainbow the last I saw of it."

Diamond believed the talking had taken the edge off Matt's alertness. He streaked for his gun.

He lost. Matt drew and fired faster.

The bullet struck Diamond in the chest. Diamond's .45 exploded but it was a dying man who had pulled the trigger. The slug went into the earth at his feet.

Diamond reeled. Matt steadied himself to

fire again, but he saw that it was not needed as Diamond fell in a writhing shambles and then gradually stilled in death.

Shagrue again made a belated and clumsy attempt to scramble from the excavation and get to his weapons.

Matt fired. The bullet hurled a wave of sand and gravel into Shagrue's face. That drove him back. He stood in the trench, his hands lifted. "Don't kill me!" he pleaded. "Please don't!"

"Pick up that shovel," Matt said. "Keep digging. There are three more express boxes in that hole, the way I understand it."

Shagrue, shaking, began going through the motions. Nancy moved in, picked up Shagrue's guns, and the one that had fallen from Diamond's hand. She kept her eyes averted from Diamond's body. She retreated, leaned against a boulder and buried her face in her hands.

Matt moved to her side and placed an arm around her. She looked up at him. "What do we do now, Bucko?" she sobbed.

"I don't know," he said. "I haven't thought that far ahead. One thing's for sure, as far as the two of us are concerned, Miss Smarty Pants. It isn't over. Not for us. This is only the beginning."

With Shagrue as a prisoner, they made their way to the railway track and flagged down the first train that came along. It was a westbound passenger run, and they soon had a score of volunteers to help carry the strongboxes and Diamond's body to the baggage car.

It was midafternoon when the train pulled into Cedar Springs. Word of what had happened had been telegraphed ahead, and they were met by Bill Varney, who had succeeded Nancy's father as sheriff of Cedar County. Also by an outpouring of Cedar Springs citizens.

"I'll take charge of this fellow," the sheriff said, placing handcuffs on Turk Shagrue. "And also of the one in the baggage car. There'll be an inquest, of course. The law will see to it that he's given decent burial."

He peered sternly at Matt. "As for you, I'm taking you to Rainbow. At once. In fact, I've ordered an engine and a special car to make the trip."

Nancy angrily turned on him. "What? You're not trying to say you're placing him under arrest."

"I sure don't aim to let him get out of my sight," the sheriff said.

"Well of all the blind, pigheaded, ungrateful—" she began.

"He's got some explainin' to do at Rainbow," Varney said.

"Such as what?" Her temper was at the explosive point.

"The damnedest thing happened up there not long ago," Varney said. "Folks on the east end of

First Chance Gulch were waked up by gunshots the other night, along with considerable other racket. They found a fella named Paul Wallford piled up along with his fancy rig, in the street. There was money spilled all over the place. Cash money. Greenbacks. Nigh onto twenty-nine thousand dollars' worth of it, give or take a hundred or so each way."

Bill Varney began to grin. Matt and Nancy gazed at each other, speechless.

"Instead of tryin' to be reasonable an' tell people what happened," Varney went on, "this Paul Wallford pulled a gun an' tried to run everybody back into their houses. It didn't work. Somebody put a bullet in his laig. Some citizen who was actin' in the best interests o' justice. Anyway Wallford's in a hospital in Rainbow."

Varney squinted at them. "He's under arrest. He told so many different stories about where the money came from I sort of figured that maybe a fellow named Bucko Battles could clear it up for us. Your name is Battles, ain't it? An' some folks call you Bucko."

Matt and Nancy began to laugh. She came to him and clung to him and they laughed until the tears came.

"How soon do we start for Rainbow?" Matt asked.

"*Pronto*," Varney said. "There's a lot of crow to be eaten by folks in Rainbow. I sent a telegram to some of the citizens a while ago. I understand they're declaring a holiday. They aim to meet me at the depot with a brass band. Me an' any prisoners I happen to fetch along."

"A brass band!" Matt moaned. "God forbid!"

"A brass band isn't half good enough," Nancy said. She linked arms with Matt. "Lead the way, Sheriff. He'll live through it. He's lived through worse."

She looked up at him and added, "But, that's nothing to what you'll go through from now on. I'll see to that, Bucko, my lad."

| Books are produced in the United States using U.S.-based materials | Books are printed using a revolutionary new process called THINKtech™ that lowers energy usage by 70% and increases overall quality | Books are durable and flexible because of Smyth-sewing | Paper is sourced using environmentally responsible foresting methods and the paper is acid-free |

Center Point Large Print
600 Brooks Road / PO Box 1
Thorndike, ME 04986-0001 USA

(207) 568-3717

US & Canada:
1 800 929-9108
www.centerpointlargeprint.com